ACCLAIM FOR COLL

"Second chances, old flames, and startling new revelations combine to form a story filled with faith, trial, forgiveness, and redemption. Crack the cover and step in, but beware—Mermaid Point is harboring secrets that will keep you guessing."

—LISA WINGATE, NATIONAL BESTSELLING
AUTHOR OF *THE SEA KEEPER'S DAUGHTERS*
ON *MERMAID MOON*

"I burned through *The Inn at Ocean's Edge* in one sitting. An intricate plot by a master storyteller. Colleen Coble has done it again with this gripping opening to a new series. I can't wait to spend more time at Sunset Cove."

—HEATHER BURCH, BESTSELLING AUTHOR OF
ONE LAVENDER RIBBON

"Coble doesn't disappoint with her custom blend of suspense and romance."

—*PUBLISHER'S WEEKLY* FOR *THE INN AT
OCEAN'S EDGE*

"Veteran author Coble has penned another winner. Filled with mystery and romance that are unpredictable until the last page, this novel will grip readers long past when they should put their books down. Recommended to readers of contemporary mysteries."

—*CBA RETAILERS + RESOURCES* REVIEW OF
THE INN AT OCEAN'S EDGE

"Coble truly shines when she's penning a mystery, and this tale will really keep the reader guessing . . . Mystery lovers will definitely want to put this book on their purchase list."

—*ROMANTIC TIMES* BOOK REVIEW OF *THE INN
AT OCEAN'S EDGE*

"Master storyteller Colleen Coble has done it again. *The Inn at Ocean's Edge* is an intricately woven, well-crafted story of romance, suspense, family secrets, and a decades old mystery. Needless to say, it had me hooked from page one. I simply couldn't stop turning the pages. This one's going on my keeper shelf."

—LYNETTE EASON, AWARD-WINNING,
BESTSELLING AUTHOR OF THE HIDDEN
IDENTITY SERIES

"Evocative and gripping, *The Inn at Ocean's Edge* will keep you flipping pages long into the night."

—DANI PETTREY, BESTSELLING AUTHOR OF
THE ALASKAN COURAGE SERIES

"Coble's atmospheric and suspenseful series launch should appeal to fans of Tracie Peterson and other authors of Christian romantic suspense."

—LIBRARY JOURNAL REVIEW OF *TIDEWATER
INN*

"Romantically tense, but with just the right touch of danger, this cowboy love story is surprisingly clever—and pleasingly sweet."

—USAToday.com REVIEW OF *BLUE MOON
PROMISE*

"Colleen Coble will keep you glued to each page as she shows you the beauty of God's most primitive land and the dangers it hides."

—WWW.ROMANCEJUNKIES.COM

"[An] outstanding, completely engaging tale that will have you on the edge of your seat . . . A must-have for all fans of romantic suspense!"

—TheRomanceReadersConnection.com
REVIEW OF *ANATHEMA*

"Colleen Coble lays an intricate trail in *Without a Trace* and draws the reader on like a hound with a scent."

—ROMANTIC TIMES, 4½ STARS

"Coble's historical series just keeps getting better with each entry."

—LIBRARY JOURNAL STARRED REVIEW OF
THE LIGHTKEEPER'S BALL

"Don't ever mistake [Coble's] for the fluffy romances with a little bit of suspense. She writes solid suspense, and she ties it all together beautifully with a wonderful message."

—LIFEINREVIEWBLOG.COM REVIEW OF
LONESTAR ANGEL

"This book has everything I enjoy: mystery, romance, and suspense. The characters are likable, understandable, and I can relate to them."

—THEFRIENDLYBOOKNOOK.COM

"[M]ystery, danger, and intrigue as well as romance, love, and subtle inspiration. *The Lightkeeper's Daughter* is a 'keeper.'"

—ONCEUPONAROMANCE.COM

"Colleen is a master storyteller."

—KAREN KINGSBURY, BESTSELLING
AUTHOR OF UNLOCKED AND LEARNING

To
LOVE A
STRANGER

Also by Colleen Coble

Sunset Cove novels
The Inn at Ocean's Edge
Mermaid Moon
Twilight at Blueberry Barrens
(Available September 2016)

Hope Beach novels
Tidewater Inn
Rosemary Cottage
Seagrass Pier
*All Is Bright: A Hope Beach
Christmas Novella (e-book only)*

Under Texas Stars novels
Blue Moon Promise
Safe in His Arms

The Mercy Falls series
The Lightkeeper's Daughter
The Lightkeeper's Bride
The Lightkeeper's Ball

Lonestar novels
Lonestar Sanctuary
Lonestar Secrets
Lonestar Homecoming
Lonestar Angel
*All Is Calm: A Lonestar
Christmas Novella (e-book only)*

The Rock Harbor series
Without a Trace
Beyond a Doubt
Into the Deep
Cry in the Night
*Silent Night: A Rock Harbor
Christmas Novella (e-book only)*

The Aloha Reef series
Distant Echoes
Black Sands
Dangerous Depths
Midnight Sea
*Holy Night: An Aloha Reef
Christmas Novella (e-book only)*

Alaska Twilight
Fire Dancer
Abomination
Anathema
Butterfly Palace

Novellas included in:
Smitten
Secretly Smitten
Smitten Book Club

Other Novellas
Bluebonnet Bride

To
LOVE A
STRANGER

A NOVEL

COLLEEN
COBLE

THOMAS NELSON
Since 1798

Published in Nashville, Tennessee, by Thomas Nelson. Thomas Nelson is a registered trademark of HarperCollins Christian Publishing, Inc.

Thomas Nelson titles may be purchased in bulk for educational, business, fundraising, or sales promotional use. For information, please e-mail SpecialMarkets@ThomasNelson.com.

Scripture quotations are from the King James Version.

Publisher's Note: This novel is a work of fiction. Names, characters, places, and incidents are either products of the author's imagination or used fictitiously. All characters are fictional, and any similarity to people living or dead is purely coincidental.

Library of Congress Cataloging-in-Publication Data

Names: Coble, Colleen, author.
Title: To love a stranger / Colleen Coble.
Description: Nashville : Thomas Nelson, [2016]
Identifiers: LCCN 2016001431 | ISBN 9780529103451 (softcover)
Subjects: LCSH: Man-woman relationships--Fiction. | GSAFD: Christian fiction. | Love stories.
Classification: LCC PS3553.O2285 T6 2016 | DDC 813/.54--dc23 LC record available at http://lccn.loc.gov/2016001431

Printed in the United States of America

16 17 18 19 20 RRD 6 5 4 3 2 1

For my beloved husband, David Coble, whose many loving qualities serve as a model for all my heroes. I love you, Dave!

Prologue

April 1868

Fort Bridger, Utah Territory

"You are not going to marry some chit you've never set eyes on, Jasper! I don't care what kind of promise you made."

Jasper Mendenhall winced at the strident tone in his sister's voice. Still, he was glad to hear her say his name in any kind of voice. Just a few months ago he was certain he had no hope of ever seeing her again. Sent to different homes from the orphanage, their reunion had seemed a lost dream. But now at long last they had found each other.

He glanced at Jessie. Her face had flushed bright with the intensity of her emotions and nearly matched her red hair. He resisted the urge to tell her to mind her own business. She was just showing sisterly apprehension, but it still grated a bit. He wasn't some callow youth. "I know her quite well, Jessie. We've been corresponding for over six months. I appreciate your concern, but I must ask you to stay out of this."

Clay Cole put a restraining hand on her arm. "Calm down, sweetheart. It's not good for the baby for you to get upset." He guided his wife to a nearby chair. Once she was seated he turned to Jasper. "I can't say I'm in favor of this idea either. What do you really know about this woman? She could say anything in a letter. What is her name again?"

"Bessie. Bessie Randall. She's twenty-six and lives in Boston."

Jessica sniffed and wrinkled her nose. "Huh! A spinster. She's probably homely as a fishwife, Jasper."

He took a picture from the pocket of his blue uniform jacket. "See for yourself." He handed the picture to Clay, who glanced at it, then gave it to Jessica.

She stared at it and sniffed again. "All right, she's beautiful, and that makes it even worse. How can you even contemplate taking a lovely young woman out to the Arizona Territory? She looks refined and gently reared. Have you even told her what kind of conditions she'll be facing at Fort Bowie? Besides, something must be wrong with her if she's so beautiful and still unmarried. That pretty face probably hides a shrew."

Jasper and Clay looked at one another and grinned.

Jessica's flushed cheeks darkened even more, and she had the grace to look embarrassed. "I can see what you're thinking. And if it was once true in my case, that just goes to prove what I was saying. Now answer my question. Did you tell her where you'll be stationed?"

Jasper shifted his gaze from her accusing glare. He hadn't

2

told Bessie everything. He wanted to surprise her. He knew her well enough from her letters to know she craved adventure and would welcome the challenge. But what if Jessica was right? Was it proper to take his beloved to such a wild and untamed place?

"I thought not." Jessica's voice held a trace of satisfaction. "Jasper, think about this before you do it. You should wait until you find the right woman. I want you to have what Clay and I have. Don't settle for second best." She sent a tender glance toward Clay, and he smiled back just as tenderly.

Jasper wanted what they had too. And he was certain he and Bessie would have that, given time. He already loved her fire and spirit, the tenderness he found in her letters. He longed for a home and children. "It's already done, Jessie."

Clay and Jessica both looked at him sharply. He shrugged and turned his head. They might as well hear it all. "She went through a proxy marriage and sent me the papers. I did the same and sent her the marriage lines and tickets last week. She's my wife, and I expect you to make her welcome when she gets here. She should be here within the month." He said the last firmly. Jessica could still be a bit of a termagant if she thought someone was taking advantage of her precious family.

She rose to her feet and stared at him. The color drained out of her face. "Jasper, what have you done?"

One

April 1868

Boston, Massachusetts

"What are you doing in my room, Bessie?"

Bessie Randall heard Lenore's shrill voice as though from a great distance. The lines of writing wavered before her eyes, and the hand that held the letter shook violently. This letter couldn't mean what it said. It just wasn't possible. She stared at the words again, then closed her eyes briefly before turning to face her sister.

She held out the letter. "What is the meaning of this, Lenore?"

Lenore's pale, lovely skin flushed. She shifted her gaze guiltily and swallowed hard. "What are you doing going through my things?" Her tone of outrage didn't ring true. Her blue eyes filled with tears, and she bit her lip.

"Don't try to change the subject. I was looking for my ostrich fan you borrowed for church last week." Bessie waved the letter in the air. "And it's a good thing I did. I never would have known about this." She desperately hoped there was some explanation other than the obvious.

Lenore gulped. "It's rather difficult to explain." She wound a raven lock around her finger and avoided Bessie's gaze.

"I should say so! There seems to be train and stage tickets here with the letter too. Tickets to Fort Bridger, Utah Territory—in *my* name." Bessie let out an incredulous laugh. Utah Territory! That was the last place she would want to go. She had heard about the Indian uprisings and bloodshed out there.

"If you would just let me explain." Lenore implored her with a pleading glance. "It started so innocently." She took a deep breath, then blurted it all out. "Jasper Mendenhall sent a letter to Marjorie's agency six months ago. I had just started volunteering there, and it seemed so romantic to help lonely bachelors in the West find mates. Jasper wanted to correspond with a young woman interested in marriage. I saw his picture and was quite taken with him."

Bessie took several deep breaths. It wouldn't do to get angry. "I knew no good would come of you helping out at that agency. Our cousin never had a lick of sense, and you can be just as bad."

Lenore colored at the reprimand. "Mother and Father would never allow me to correspond with a man, especially a soldier . . . so I used your name." She wrung her hands and turned away from Bessie's glare. "I know it was wrong, but it seemed harmless at the time. I intended to break it off. Truly, I did. But it just escalated. He asked me to go through a proxy marriage and join him. It sounded so exciting, Bessie. I didn't think. I just did it."

She turned back and stared at Bessie with pleading eyes. "You know how I've longed for adventure, how I've dreamed of going West."

"But this, Lenore!" Bessie's heart pounded, and dread congealed in her stomach. She didn't want to think about this tangle or how on earth she would get her madcap sister out of this scrap. Their very proper parents would be horrified. They guarded their society status above all else.

Lenore slid an anxious glance at her. "Since then I met Richard. I want to be with him, not some man I've never met."

Lenore had done some thoughtless things, but this was beyond the pale. To lead a man on like this—and a soldier serving his country, no less! Despicable. Tears burned in Bessie's eyes. Would Lenore never learn to think before she leapt into things? "Are you telling me that you married this man? And falsely, too, since you aren't Bessie Randall."

Lenore couldn't meet her gaze. "No, Bessie. It means you are married to Jasper. If you contest it, I–I think I could be arrested for forging your name."

Bessie gasped. The strength ran from her legs, and she sat on the bed. Taking a deep breath, she looked from her sister back down to the tickets and the letter. She drew another shuddering breath. How was she to extricate Lenore and herself from this predicament? "I see. You didn't want to marry a man you've never met, but you've married *me* to someone I've never heard of before today." She hugged herself. "What am I to do?" she whispered. "What can be done?"

"Please don't tell Mother and Father about this. Father said if I

7

got in any more trouble, he would ship me off to Uncle Matthew's in Rhode Island. I can't leave now that I've met Richard. I intend to marry him."

Did Lenore ever think of anyone but herself? Bessie loved her younger sister, but this was too much. She didn't know if she could forgive her for this. "How could you, Lenore? How could you bind me to some man I've never met?" Her thoughts raced, trying to uncover a plan, any plan, to unravel this tangle.

Lenore burst into noisy sobs. "You hate me!"

Bessie pressed her fingers between her eyes where the persistent throbbing pulsed. "Oh, do hush, Lenore, and let me think."

Her sister's sobs tapered off, but Bessie could still feel her anxious gaze. Lenore turned away finally and began to fuss with her hair. Bessie stared at her sister. She was so lovely. Translucent skin, thick black hair, and full lips that drew men like bees to honey.

Bessie's own hair was merely mousy brown, and the rest of her features were only echoes of Lenore's beauty. Lenore had beaus by the dozen, and Bessie had yet to receive her first proposal of marriage. And she might never receive one. She wasn't ugly. Just ordinary. Quiet and ordinary.

Lenore turned from the looking glass and gave her a coaxing smile. "I know you would like Jasper. And you'd make a much better soldier's wife than I would." She crossed the room and sat on the bed beside Bessie. "You know Father says I shall not be allowed to marry until you do. What if you never marry? Richard may weary of waiting for me." She bit her lip, and tears hung on her lashes. "I don't mean to be cruel, but you're already twenty-six. Perhaps this is your opportunity."

Perhaps it was. How picky could Jasper be if he was willing to marry by proxy? Maybe he wouldn't really be expecting a beauty. Simply a wife. He was expecting Bessie Randall, and she was Bessie Randall, not Lenore. If she didn't go, she would be breaking a promise made in her name. Her reputation and honor would be smirched.

She supposed the marriage could be annulled or whatever one did in this kind of situation, but she had to be honest with herself. She longed for a husband and children of her own. Lately she had questioned whether it would ever happen—or if she would die a spinster.

"I shall never marry a nonbeliever, Lenore. What of this Jasper? Have you inquired about his faith?" That was the most important thing. She could deal with other problems, but marriage to a nonbeliever would be intolerable.

Her sister brightened. "Indeed I did. Jasper is a fine Christian man. His brother-in-law is a minister at Fort Bridger." Hope gave a sparkle to her eyes.

A minister's brother-in-law. It sounded good. Bessie pressed her fingers against the bridge of her nose again. Was this the Lord's will for her? She couldn't decide now. "I shall pray about it, Lenore. Say nothing to our parents until I make my decision." She started toward the door, then hesitated. "Have you a picture of this man? And might I see a letter or two?" Not that his looks were really important, but ill humor often showed in the expression.

"Of course." Lenore hastened to her dressing table and opened her jewel box. She extracted a photo and a bundle of letters tied with pink ribbon. "He is really a very nice man, Bessie. I think the two of you would deal splendidly together."

Bessie took the packet of letters and the photograph. "I shall be the judge of that, Lenore. Your judgment leaves much to be desired." She hardened her heart against the hurt expression on her sister's face and hurried to her own room.

After she shut the door behind her, Bessie opened the balcony door and stepped onto the small porch overlooking the ocean. Settling onto the single chair, she turned her attention first to the photograph. Jasper was not what Bessie would call handsome, but his face was interesting. A nose a bit too large for his face with a hump in the middle as though it had been broken, thick brows, and a square jaw gave his face character. And there seemed to be a bit of humor in his eyes and in the tilt of his lips. The rapid pace of her heart stilled a bit. Character was all-important. She laid the photo on the table, then untied the ribbon on the letters. She began with the oldest.

By the time she was halfway through the letters, she knew she had to go. She could not disappoint this man. She had a heart of love to give, and this man seemed willing to accept a wife with open arms. Besides, the deed was already done. She was bound to this man, and she would see it through. If he chose to put her away once he saw her, that decision would be upon his head. She would go West.

Jasper paced the rough boardwalk outside the stage depot. The stage was never on time, and today was no exception. It should have arrived early this morning, and here it was nearly five. His heart pounded at the thought of finally meeting his lovely bride. Her letters had filled him with delight, for she had a fire and passion for life. He flipped open the cover from his pocket watch again, then sighed, closed it, and slipped the watch back inside his pocket.

Stepping into the street, he looked down the rough trail to the east. Was that a cloud of dust? Shading his eyes with one hand, he squinted. It was the stage. He stepped back onto the boardwalk and slapped the dust from his breeches with his hat. What would Bessie think when she saw him? Would she be disappointed?

The lathered horses stopped in front of him, and the stagecoach driver began to toss luggage from the top of the stage to the numerous waiting hands. Someone opened the stage door, and the passengers began to disembark. A corpulent man with a handlebar mustache climbed out first, while the stage springs groaned in protest at his weight. Next came an older woman with a baby in her arms, followed by a slight young woman in drab brown.

Jasper waited eagerly for several minutes, but no one else exited. He approached the stage door and peered in: two men in black suits were the only occupants. His heart fell. She didn't come. Her telegram had said she would be on this stage. He felt a stab of alarm. Was she all right?

The young woman in brown averted her eyes when he turned back around. She had been staring at him, and the flush on her cheeks told Jasper she was aware of her bad manners. He had to pass her to reach the telegraph office next to the stage depot, and she cleared her throat when he reached her side.

"Excuse me, sir. Are you—?" She raised grave eyes and searched his face. "Are you Jasper Mendenhall?"

He stared down at her. She was a tiny thing, barely five feet tall, and slightly built. She wore a striking hat with an ostrich feather that dangled over one eye, but such an elegant hat looked out of place on such an ordinary woman. A tendril of light-brown hair had escaped its pins and straggled against her pale cheek. Her gray eyes appeared enormous in her pinched face.

How did she know his name? A sense of unease swept over him. "Yes, ma'am. I'm Jasper Mendenhall. May I assist you in some way?"

Her lips trembled, and her face became even more colorless. She swallowed hard. "I–I'm Bessie. B–Bessie Mendenhall. Your wife."

Jasper blinked and then the breath left his lungs. This couldn't be his Bessie! His Bessie was vibrant with life. She was dark and striking. She wasn't this little mouse of a woman. Was this some kind of terrible joke?

She must have seen his shock, and tears flooded her gray eyes. She fished in her reticule but couldn't seem to find what she was looking for. "I am so sorry," she whispered. "Have you a handkerchief?"

Dazed, he pulled one from his pocket and handed it to her.

He looked her over again, trying to find some resemblance to the photo he carried next to his heart. Perhaps the nose and mouth were similar?

She dabbed her cheeks, then straightened slim shoulders and craned her head to look into his face. "Is there someplace more private we can go to discuss this matter?"

Still speechless, he nodded. He was afraid to say anything. The hot, clamoring words rushing through his head would crush this pale creature. But he longed to shout them. Duped. He'd been duped. Jessica and Clay had been right. How could he have been so foolish? He thought he knew his Bessie, but he was obviously wrong. As he led the way down the street to Clay's church, he couldn't bear to look at her.

When he realized Bessie was nearly running to keep up with his long stride, he slowed his pace and offered her his arm. The touch of her hand on his arm was loathsome, but he forced himself to accept it. What kind of woman would deceive a man the way she'd done? Contempt curled his lip, but he kept his mouth clamped shut. He didn't dare give vent to his feelings.

He opened the church door and ushered her into the cool interior. The calming atmosphere had an immediate effect on his temper. His breathing slowed, and he seated her in a pew and stood gazing down at her.

She fiddled with the tassels on her reticule. "I know how this looks."

"Do you?"

She glanced up at his tight words. "Please, sit down. You'll give me a crick in my neck. You're very tall. Taller than I expected."

He sat beside her. "And you're not at all as I expected you."

She bit her lip. "I know. You were expecting Lenore. I didn't think to ask if she'd sent a picture of herself. When I saw your reaction, I knew she had."

"What on earth are you talking about? Who is Lenore? I don't understand anything except the fact that you deceived me."

She laid a small hand on his arm, and he had to resist the impulse to shake it off. "Lenore is my sister. My baby sister. She's twenty-one and should have known better, but she's the one who has been writing to you, using my name. I discovered these contretemps by accident, and I have come to honor the promise made in my name."

He stared into her face. Had she seriously thought that she could take the place of her lovely sister? Did she think him so desperate he would marry a bride sight unseen? Why hadn't this sister she called Lenore come? Twenty-one was of an age for marriage.

"I know how it looks." She stared down at her lap, pleating the folds of her dusty brown dress.

"I don't think you do. If you did, you wouldn't have come. You would have written and explained the situation and given me the chance to set this tangle straight. Did you think that one woman was the same as the next to me?"

"Well . . . you did write to the agency looking for a wife."

"Yes, but I had the opportunity to choose for myself." He squeezed his hands into fists. "You had a picture of me, didn't you?"

She nodded uncertainly.

"How would you have felt if you arrived and found you'd married a man of fifty with gray hair and whiskers?"

Bessie's face whitened as his words penetrated. "I see what you mean," she said softly. "You are displeased with my appearance." Tears swam in her eyes again. "Please forgive me, Lieutenant. If I'd realized you had a picture of Lenore, I can assure you I never would have come unannounced this way."

He folded his arms across his chest. "I find that hard to believe, Miss Randall." She had trapped him. Perhaps her younger sister had done it deliberately, since it was obvious she had to have known what her sister was doing.

"Mrs. Mendenhall," she corrected softly. "We are legally wed. That is why I have come."

Jasper stared at her. He wanted to groan in frustration. How could he unravel this mess? "That may be true, but under the circumstances, we may not be wed long. I will consult an attorney as soon as I can and see just where we stand."

Her face paled even more, if that were possible. "You would send me home?"

He sighed and rubbed his chin. Against his will, pity stirred his heart. Perhaps this monstrous trick was not her doing. She didn't seem conniving enough for such a scheme. "You must be tired. Let me take you to my sister's home. She likely has supper waiting."

Two

Bessie saw every knothole, every nail in the boardwalk as she followed her new husband across the fort to meet his family. New husband. What if he set the marriage aside? What if she had come all this way only to be sent back in disgrace? He had done nothing to endear himself to her, but she couldn't bear the thought of going back to Boston. What would people think?

Fort Bridger bustled with activity. Men tipped their hats at her as they passed on the wide boardwalk, and several women stared inquisitively at her. They seemed especially taken with her hat. It was new and the height of fashion, but Bessie wanted to fling the hat away so she could creep through the fort without being noticed. Did they all know Jasper was expecting a beautiful wife?

"Jasper!"

She turned at the sound of a feminine voice. A young woman stepped from the nearby general store and waved her hand in their direction.

"Miriam." Jasper tipped his hat at the vision in blue.

Her hat was perched atop a cluster of dark curls, and her gown, although last year's fashion, enhanced her slim figure. Bessie smiled at her uncertainly.

"Bessie, this is my cousin Miriam," Jasper said.

Miriam tapped him on the arm with her fan. "Why do you insist on pretending we are related?" She pouted. "Jessica is my cousin only by adoption. You and I are not."

"Miriam, I'd like you to meet Bessie, my wife."

Miriam's eyes widened, and she shot a venomous glare at Bessie. Then her gray eyes filled with tears, and she took a step back. She whirled and practically ran down the boardwalk.

"She cares for you." Bessie felt sorry for the girl.

Jasper sighed. "Perhaps, but the feeling is not mutual. She is too much like a younger sister. I never intended to hurt her, though."

He sounded grieved. Jasper had a softer heart than she had imagined. Heartened, she took his arm again, and they continued down the boardwalk. All the air left her chest at the thought of meeting his family. They would surely be just as astonished at her appearance as Jasper had been. Her heart fluttered in her chest like a frightened bird. At least he hadn't denounced her and cast her off at first sight, but she had seen the disappointment in his eyes when he looked at her. And who could blame him? Lenore was a scarlet cardinal—she was a brown wren.

She drew her shawl around her shoulders to ward off both the chill of the wind and the coldness of his rejection. Had she really expected he would take one look at her and forget Lenore? She blinked back tears and squared her shoulders. She might not be a beauty, but there was more to being a good wife than beauty, wasn't there? Or was that truly the only important thing to men? She hadn't had enough experience to know.

Fort Bridger was an attractive place. The walk they were on led past neatly whitewashed homes with wide front porches and small yards with spring flowers poking up through the soil. Bessie liked what she saw. It was so different from Boston. Small and quaint as if they'd stepped back to a gentler time. They stopped outside a small, whitewashed cabin with a curl of smoke escaping from the chimney. The front stoop was barely large enough for them both to stand on.

Jasper rapped once on the door, then pushed it open. "Jessica, we're here."

The tantalizing aroma of beef stew wafted down the hall, and Bessie's stomach rumbled. The fare had been poor on the stage route, and she'd eaten mostly hard bread and bits of salt pork. Now she was suddenly ravenous.

A lovely red-haired woman hurried toward them. The gentle bulge under her skirt proclaimed the arrival of a new baby in a few months. She had to be Jasper's sister. They both had those vivid blue eyes that tilted up at the corners. Her smile was welcoming, but it seemed to hold a touch of reserve at the same time.

She looked at Bessie, then turned to Jasper with a question in her eyes.

He cleared his throat. "Jessica, this is Bessie. Bessie, my sister, Jessica."

Jessica's mouth dropped open, but she quickly recovered and

held out her hand. "Welcome, Bessie. I always wanted a sister. I look forward to getting acquainted. Come into the kitchen. We're about to sit down for supper, but we were waiting for you."

Bessie could sense the discomfort emanating from her husband. He hadn't introduced her as his wife. She had to wonder why, when he had told Miriam. Obviously Jessica had seen the picture of Lenore as well. Oh, why hadn't she thought to ask Lenore if she had sent a photograph? Tears pricked the backs of her eyes, but she forced them away. She would take one step at a time.

A dark-haired giant of a man stood when they came through the door. Unlike his wife's, his welcoming smile held no trace of surprise or wariness. Bessie warmed to him instantly.

"So, this is my new sister! Welcome to Fort Bridger, Bessie." His large hand enveloped hers.

A little blonde girl was seated at the far end of the table. "Hello. My name is Franny. What's yours? I'm three."

Bessie smiled at her in relief. She loved children. "I'm Bessie." She wanted to tell the child she was her new aunt, but what if Jasper didn't let her stay? "I'm very glad to meet you, Franny. I've heard lots about you from your uncle Jasper."

She sensed his start of surprise and realized how her words sounded. Like she had been corresponding with him. He would be convinced she had been a part of the deception.

Jessica interrupted before she could continue. "Sit down. You can tell us all about yourself over supper."

Bessie slid reluctantly into the seat beside Franny, and Jasper sat beside her. In spite of her hunger, she didn't know how she could force a morsel of food down with all of them looking at her.

Clay said grace, then passed around the stew. "Have you always lived in Boston?"

Bessie nodded. "All my life. This is very different from what I'm used to. It's lovely, though. Even the terrain looks wild and untamed."

Jessica glanced at her brother. "So you two have been writing to one another over six months, Jasper says. I must say, you don't look quite like your picture."

Bessie gulped and drew a deep breath. What should she say? The silence drew out for a long moment before Jasper cleared his throat.

"I mistakenly showed you a picture of Bessie's sister, Lenore." He turned to his brother-in-law. "Did you hear about the Sioux attack up north yesterday?"

Bessie was glad to let the men talk while she gathered her composure. Her cheeks burned with mortification, and she could barely hold the tears at bay. She thought she had done the right thing to come, but now she would give anything to be back in her home in Boston. This tangle became worse every moment. At least Jasper had made it seem as though it was his fault about the picture. That was kind of him. She sent him a smile, and he smiled briefly before he frowned and turned away.

She was aware of Jessica's probing gaze all through dinner, and although it was kindly, it still discomfited her. She knew her sister-in-law was full of questions. After supper the men retired to the parlor while she helped Jessica clear away the supper dishes. Franny helped them and kept up a steady chatter. Bessie was thankful for the distraction—she dreaded more questions from Jessica.

Just before they joined the men, Jessica put her hand on Bessie's arm. "I don't quite know what's gone on in this courtship, but I want to tell you I think you'll be very good for Jasper." She hesitated, then continued with a sparkle in her eyes. "I was afraid he was getting some hothouse society beauty from the East who would lead him on a merry chase. If there's ever anything I can do to help, just ask. I'm here for you both."

Bessie lost the struggle against her tears. "Thank you, Jessica. I'll do my best to be a good wife." She struggled to stifle her sobs. What would Jasper think if he came in and saw her crying to his sister? He would despise her all the more.

"My goodness, don't cry. Jasper will think I've been asking nosy questions in here, and Clay will scold me." She gave her a handkerchief. "Things will work out. Do your best and trust God for the rest."

"Thank you," Bessie managed.

When the women entered the parlor, Clay smiled at his wife and patted the seat beside him on the threadbare sofa. Jasper gave Bessie a stiff smile and moved over so she could join him on the settee. She sat gingerly on the edge and tried not to crowd him too much. This was the closest she had been to him since she arrived, and a flush warmed her cheeks.

"I have some news for all of you," he announced once they'd all gotten settled. "The column leaves for Fort Bowie Tuesday."

"No, Jasper, not so soon!" Jessica wailed. "We haven't had enough time to get reacquainted, and Bessie and I have hardly even had a chance to talk."

Bessie looked from her new husband to Jessica then back again. What did he mean? Where was Fort Bowie?

He turned toward her. "I've been reassigned to Fort Bowie, Arizona Territory."

Bessie felt light-headed. Apaches were in the Arizona Territory. She had heard many stories about the feared Indians. Did he expect her to go into a place like that? She would just refuse. She could either go home or stay here until he returned. He questioned the truth of their marriage anyway. She opened her mouth to tell him so, but Jessica beat him to it.

"You can't take Bessie there."

"Bessie came all this way for a husband. I don't imagine she would allow me to leave her behind."

Was that a touch of mockery in his voice? He surely didn't really want her to go, did he? This would be the perfect opportunity for him to get rid of her. He smiled, a slight upturn of his firm lips, but his expression convinced Bessie. If this marriage had any hope at all, she had to try. She knew he still questioned her motives, but perhaps on the long trip to Arizona Territory, she would have a chance to answer his doubts.

The candles had burned low by the time Jasper stood and

announced it was time for bed. Bessie's heavy eyelids popped open at the mention of bed. Where was she to sleep? She couldn't share a bed with him yet. She just couldn't. Since he questioned the marriage, he surely didn't expect her to. Her mouth dry, she clenched her fists in the folds of her dress and frantically tried to think of an excuse.

"I've put a bed in the hall for Bessie, Jasper. Are you staying at Officers' Row for now?" Jessica asked.

He nodded. "There was no reason to request quarters for just a few days." He laid a hand on her shoulder. "I'll see you in the morning."

Bessie breathed a sigh of relief when he turned and left the house. At least God had spared her that problem.

"I expect you're exhausted. Let me show you to your bed."

Jessica showed Bessie to her tiny curtained-off alcove in the hall and left her alone. Bessie sat on the edge of the bed and took off her ridiculous hat. She disrobed quickly and pulled her night-gown on, glad to be alone even though lonely tears burned her eyes. She missed her large room with the familiar quilt her grandmother made.

Why hadn't she told her parents the entire story? Her father would have found some way to fix it. Instead she had allowed herself to be swayed by her sister's tears and her own thoughts of a husband and children. At this moment she saw no way she and Jasper would ever have the kind of marriage she'd hoped to have. If Lenore had been here, she could have cheerfully throttled her.

Ever since Lenore was born, Bessie had been compared to her lovely sister. Bessie longed for someone to love her, to think she was wonderful. If she had only known Jasper had seen a picture of Lenore, she would have handled this very differently.

She squeezed her eyes shut. *Please, Lord. Please make him love me.* It was her last thought before the long trip took its toll and sleep claimed her.

❧

She awoke to the sounds of bugles and the shouts of men. Her eyes felt gritty, and she was reluctant to leave the warmth of her bed. For a moment she wondered where she was, until she heard a deep voice call, "Six o'clock and all's well."

She was at Fort Bridger, and all was not well. Her new husband and his family would be looking her over again today. She sighed and sat up. Today was a new day, a fresh start. Lenore would have given up and gone home, but Bessie hadn't come this far to turn tail and run. She had always stayed in the background, but this was her only opportunity to prove to herself and to Jasper that she could be a good wife. Gathering her courage, she slipped out of bed and quickly washed. She pulled on a blue chintz dress, then pushed aside the blankets that curtained off her partition.

Her new husband sat beside the fire with Franny on his lap. Bessie could smell the aroma of coffee and fresh-made bread. For just an instant she fantasized that this was her home and Franny was her daughter. Her face burned at the thought.

Jasper was dressed in his blue uniform, his red hair slicked down with hair tonic. Bessie thought he looked very appealing. Strong and competent. His broad shoulders filled out his jacket nicely, and the tenderness in his face when he looked at Franny tugged at Bessie's heartstrings. Would he ever look at her like that?

Jasper looked up, and his gaze locked with hers. A slight hint of color rose on his cheeks.

He stood and set Franny on her feet. "Run tell Mama that Bessie is ready for her breakfast." He continued to regard her gravely for a moment. "Did you sleep well?"

"I don't remember." She smiled.

He grinned. "That's a good sign."

They stared at one another for a long moment, then Bessie's face went hot and she looked down at her hands. "When do we leave for Arizona Territory?"

"Actually, the departure has been moved up. We leave tomorrow." His blue eyes searched her face. "Are you sure you want to do this, Bessie? I have to be honest. It's a hard place to live. You seem—" He broke off and looked away.

"I seem what?"

His gaze caught hers again. "Frail, timid, shy. I'm not at all sure you are up to the challenge."

She pressed her lips together. Appearances could be deceiving. Would a frail, timid woman even have come this far? She thought not. "Why are you saying this now? Why didn't you mention it in your letters?"

"The Bessie I thought I knew would have relished the challenge. I wanted to surprise her."

Her temper flared at the condescension in his tone. "I'm not the frail bird you seem to think I am. I may be small and plain, but I have grit and determination. I can see you're disappointed, but you're not what I expected either. Your letters seemed to reveal a man with humor and good nature."

Jasper raised an eyebrow. "I never deceived you, I mean, Lenore. I never pretended to be someone I was not."

"I didn't either. The deed was done by the time I found out about it. What do you intend? Divorce?"

The ugly word hung in the air between them. "It might be an annulment," he said slowly. "When we reach Arizona Territory, I'll consult an attorney and see where we stand. We can then make a decision on what to do." He smiled. "If you're with me, at least I'll have someone to talk to when the wolves are howling outside the door and the scorpions are trying to get in."

She felt faint at the word picture he drew. Then she saw the mirth in his eyes and realized he was teasing. She sent him a feeble grin. "I shall just invite them in for supper. That will frighten them away."

A look of surprise raced across his face. "Is your cooking that bad?"

"Well, let me put it this way. Indigestion would be the least of your worries."

He laughed, and Bessie liked the sound of his deep chuckle.

"We'll get along somehow. I'm a pretty fair cook myself." His smile faded, and he turned toward the door. "Be ready to leave at six."

She nodded and watched him leave. This was her first glimpse of the humor and wit she had seen in his letters. But what did it matter if he intended to find a way out of their marriage? She went to the kitchen to find some breakfast.

Jessica smiled in welcome. "Are you hungry? There's hot coffee and bread with jam."

"I'd love some. I'm famished." Bessie sat at the table and took the cup of coffee Jessica handed her. She was already beginning to feel Jessica could be a friend. She spread some blackberry jam on a slice of warm bread and bit into it, but her hands trembled.

Jessica sat beside her. "What's wrong? You seem distressed."

Bessie took a sip of coffee. "Everything is so new and strange."

"I felt the same way." Jessica hesitated and her gaze probed Bessie's face. "But I feel you're upset about something more. Do you want to talk about it?"

Bessie longed to pour her heart out to this woman, but her loyalties would lie with her brother. She shook her head. "I'll be fine in a few days. I thank you for caring, though."

"I want to help, if I can. I've so recently found Jasper, I want to do all in my power to ensure his happiness. And yours, too, of course."

"What do you mean you recently found Jasper? The two of you seem so close."

Jessica ran her hand over the gentle swell of her belly. "Our mother died when we were small, and we were adopted by different families. Neither of us knew what had happened to the other. Clay knew I had a brother and decided he would find him and surprise me. Clay's mother supported an orphanage in Texas and had some connections with the one in Ohio where Jasper and I were taken. Clay's mother had made some inquiries for him and found out Jasper's new name. Clay then tracked him down. He was stationed at Fort Laramie when Clay contacted him. At our wedding he was waiting at the altar as Clay's best man. It was the most wonderful surprise of my life." Her eyes were misty with remembered emotion.

Tears filled Bessie's eyes. Perhaps that was why Jasper was willing to take a mail-order bride: he had been deprived of a loving home when he was small, and now he craved a family and stability. Lenore wouldn't have been capable of the selfless love Jasper needed—but Bessie was. She knew she could fill the void in his heart, if he would only let her in.

Three

The horses and wagons kicked up so much dust in the parade ground, Jasper could barely see. He glanced back and saw his new wife peering from the back of the covered ambulance wagon. Her small, pinched face was pale with fright, and she clung to the side of the ambulance with white fingers.

His lips tightened. Her terror did not bode well for the rest of the trip. He should have sent her back to Boston. Let her family untangle this mess. If the noise and commotion frightened her now, what would she be like in the wilderness of Arizona Territory? He wasn't sure he wanted to find out.

But she had shown more grit than he had expected. He thought she would insist on staying with Jessica or going back to Boston. Jessica seemed quite taken with her. She had even sent her precious seed packets along for Bessie. Jasper would withhold judgment until he got to know Bessie better. And he had to admit he wanted to get to know her.

She was no beauty, but she was attractive in a quiet sort of way. And something about her spirit drew him. Some indefinable integrity was in her eyes—which was strange, considering how she had come to be his wife. But he didn't want to think of that. It hurt to know the woman he had thought he loved had duped him like that.

He dug his heels into his mare's flank and cantered back to the ambulance. Bessie smiled when he stopped beside it, and his spirits lifted.

"You doing okay?" he shouted above the commotion.

She nodded. "Are we leaving soon?"

"Any minute."

A wave of pity for her washed over him. What was he doing dragging a frail woman like Bessie to the deprivation they faced? "You can stay here with Jessica, if you want. At least until I see what Arizona Territory is like. I can decide what to do and let you know later."

Alarm raced over her features, and she shook her head. "I shall go with you."

"As you wish." He looked to the front of the column as the band struck up the familiar departure tune of "The Girl I Left Behind Me." He tipped his hat to her and wheeled his horse to fall in line with the rest of the officers. The die was cast now. It was too late to change anything. Bessie would just have to make the best of it.

Bessie clung to the side of the wagon as the conveyance lurched its way across the trail. She hadn't seen much of Jasper since they started. She was the only woman traveling with the column, and the commander had graciously allowed her to make the ambulance her home for the trip. She shared it with an occasional soldier sent over for ointment for his feet or some such minor complaint, but for the most part, she was alone. Doctor Richter rode his horse and only stopped in if his services were needed.

She was thankful to not have to sleep on the ground. At night the wagons were put into a protective circle and tents were quickly erected. She had shuddered when she heard that several rattlesnakes were killed every night.

The spring sunshine brightened her spirits, and when the detachment stopped for a break, she decided she would walk a bit. She could use the exercise since they had been on the trail a week now. Besides, she was lonely.

She climbed down from the back of the wagon and tied her bonnet firmly under her chin. The band started its familiar tune, and the column moved forward. She walked briskly along, but she soon began to cough from the dust.

She was about to give in and get back in the ambulance when Jasper cantered up to her side. "Tired of the wagon?"

"There are no springs in that thing. And no one with whom to talk."

His blue eyes looked her over and then he sighed. "You want to ride with me awhile? I can search for a spare horse."

His sigh stung, but she was determined not to go back to the wagon yet. Besides, how could they ever hope to make something of their marriage if they never spent any time together?

"I'd like that." She had never ridden a horse before, but she wasn't about to tell him that. It would just reinforce his opinion that she was a frail, useless female. And how hard could it be to ride a horse, anyway? It looked easy enough.

He nodded and left her. A few minutes later he returned with a golden-colored horse with black markings. She thought it was called a buckskin.

"Hop on," he told her. "We don't have a sidesaddle, but I think your skirt is full enough to allow you to straddle modestly."

She eyed the stirrups. Hop on? How exactly did one do that? The horse was so big. Her head barely came to the top of its back. Tentatively she grasped the pommel and forced her boot into the stirrup. She heaved her weight up till she stood in the stirrup. Unfortunately she didn't have the least idea how to get into the saddle from there. She glanced at Jasper, and the corners of his mouth twitched.

"Wrong foot," he said gently. "You've never ridden before, have you?"

She felt the tide of heat on her cheeks and averted her gaze. She wasn't about to admit anything to a man who would laugh at her predicament. "I think I'll go back to the wagon after all," she muttered. She eased down, feeling for solid ground with the toe of her boot.

"I don't think so. I got this horse for you, and now you're going to ride her. Put your other foot in the stirrup and try again." He slid to the ground and tied his reins to the side of the ambulance wagon. "I'll help you."

Bessie bit her lip and put her right foot into the stirrup. She pulled up again, and Jasper grasped her around the waist and helped her slide her right leg across the saddle. He seemed to touch her so matter-of-factly, but the warmth of his fingers brought heat to her cheeks.

He rearranged her skirt to make sure her legs were covered. "That wasn't so hard, was it?" He handed her the reins. "Think you can handle it from here?"

"Of course." What should she do with the reins? She would not ask Jasper. He already thought she was useless. Suddenly dizzy at the height, she clutched the reins and swallowed hard. She hadn't realized a horse was so tall. What if she fell off? But if Lenore could ride, Bessie could too. She tried to remember how she had seen her sister handle the reins and moved them experimentally.

Jasper jogged ahead and caught the wagon. He untied his horse and swung into the saddle. "Follow me, and we'll go to the head to get out of this dust!" he shouted above the racket of wagons and horses. He wheeled his horse and started toward the front of the column.

Bessie tried to follow, but her horse didn't want to go in that direction. The mare tossed her head and jerked the reins from her hands, then took off at a dead run toward a grove of trees to the left of the wagons. Clinging to the pommel with both hands, she was jarred and jerked on the back of the mare. She was going to go flying off at any moment.

Would death be painful? She would find out soon enough. Frightened, all she could pray was a whispered, "Jesus, help me."

She thought she heard Jasper shout behind her, but she wasn't sure. She was going to die. The trees closed in on her, and she shut her eyes. Before the tree limbs could crash into her, Jasper shouted, "I've got you! Kick your feet free of the stirrups!"

She opened her eyes and hunched farther up the neck of her mare. She managed to work her boots free of the stirrups, then turned to look at Jasper. Leaning out of the saddle toward her, his hand grasped for the reins and missed. Then his arm snaked around her waist, and he dragged her from the saddle and across his lap.

In the ignominious position of lying facedown across his saddle, she clutched his leg with both hands. The sweaty horse hair under her cheek made her wrinkle her nose, but she was too thankful to be alive to complain about the odor or her position.

"Whoa." Jasper pulled his horse to a stop.

Bessie took a deep breath and struggled to sit up, but she was trapped with the pommel digging into her stomach. Firm hands grasped her shoulders, flipped her over, and sat her up. There was little room for both of them in the saddle, and she was forced to hang on to him as he stared into her face.

"You could have been killed!" Dust streaked his face, red spots of color marked his cheeks, and his blue eyes threw out sparks.

She coughed dust from her lungs. She had lost her bonnet somewhere, and her hair hung down her back and in her face. With trembling hands, she pushed strands of hair out of her eyes. She looked around and saw her mare drinking from the river under the trees.

Jasper glowered at her. She hated for anyone to be angry with her. Perhaps a little humor would defuse him. She tried a tentative smile. "Chirk up. I was just taking my horse for a drink. She got a little eager, but there was no need to overreact."

He stared at her, and his lips twitched. She smiled again, and his grin broadened. He pulled her against his chest and rested his chin on her head. The thud of his heart pounded under her ear, and she breathed in the musky male scent of him. When he pulled her away, she felt suddenly bereft.

He shook her gently. "I'm sorry I got so angry. It was really my fault. I should have led your horse. You look a little peaked. You sure you're all right?"

"I will be if I can just lean against your chest again."

He laughed. "I think you got knocked on the head. You're behaving a bit strangely."

She never imagined she could be so bold. Maybe she had been hit on the head. Maybe they could just stay like this forever.

He cupped her cheek, and she thought he would kiss her. But he jerked his hand away at a shout from the column.

"Lieutenant! Indians ahead!" A private waved to him from near the trees.

"Get the horse!" Jasper shouted at the private.

Bessie cowered against his chest. Indians! Her mouth dry with dread, she gripped his shirt and buried her face against him. He clutched her to his chest and urged his horse to a run.

She raised her head as they reached the wagons. The commander had already ordered the troops to move the wagons into a protective circle. They stopped at the ambulance, and Jasper handed her down to another soldier.

"Get her to safety," he told the sergeant. He looked for a long moment into her eyes, then wheeled his horse and dashed away.

Bessie watched until he was lost from sight in the milling horses and men. Sergeant Crandall hurried her under the ambulance and covered her with a blanket. He lay on his belly beside her with his gun ready. Within moments unnerving shrieks rent the air, and Bessie cowered and tried to look invisible. She had heard of the cries Indians made in battle, but she never thought she would hear them herself.

She buried her head in her arms. *Keep him safe, Lord. Don't take him when we're just now starting to get to know one another.*

The battle seemed to rage forever, then suddenly the shrieks died away until the only sounds were the shouts of the soldiers and the sharp reports of the cavalry rifles.

She got to her knees and began to crawl from under the blanket.

"Wait, Missus Mendenhall. I'm not sure it's safe yet."

"I've got to see if my husband is all right." Bessie climbed out from under the wagon. She just wanted to look into Jasper's blue eyes again.

Pandemonium reigned in the camp. Doctor Richter motioned her over. "I have wounded and need your help."

She tried to protest—she had to find Jasper—but she had no choice but to follow the doctor into the ambulance. It seemed like hours that she held compresses to bleeding wounds and soothed pain-wracked soldiers. They all seemed to still at her ministrations, and Doctor Richter told her she had a healing touch.

When the last one had been tended to, she washed the blood from her hands and climbed out of the ambulance. Where was Jasper? At least he hadn't been among the wounded. But was he among the dead?

Her hair still hung down her back, and she knew she was a dreadful sight, but she didn't care. She had to find Jasper. Everywhere she looked she saw overturned wagons and crowds of soldiers standing around discussing the battle. When she asked several soldiers if they had seen Lieutenant Jasper Mendenhall, no one seemed to know where he was. She was beginning to panic when she caught sight of his familiar red hair.

He stood talking to a group of officers. His hat was missing, and he was dirty, but he seemed to be in one piece. Bessie paused, uncertain about disturbing him when he seemed to be busy. Then one of the soldiers nodded in her direction, and he turned and their gazes locked. She saw the same concern she felt mirrored in his eyes.

He smiled then and hurried toward her. "I heard you were assisting the doctor with the wounded. It was good of you to help." He took her hands.

She clung to his fingers. The touch of his warm hands calmed her, and a sense of belonging swept over her. The thought frightened her, but she pushed it away. This felt right. As though God had put his hand of blessing on them. Maybe they would find their way yet.

"You're shivering." He took off his jacket and put it around her shoulders. Guiding her in the direction of the ambulance, Jasper took her hand and walked with her. When they reached the ambulance, he peered inside. "I'm not sure where you'll be able to sleep tonight." He paused and looked down at her. "You could stay in my tent."

Her heart pounded in her throat at his words. In his tent? What did that mean? What did he expect? Was he ready to accept their marriage as true and binding?

As though he could read her thoughts, he brushed his knuckles against her chin and gazed into her eyes. "No strings. I'll get an extra cot. It will give us a chance to get better acquainted."

Wasn't that what she wanted? Then why was she so afraid? She swallowed her fear and nodded. "I'll get my things."

Four

Jasper pushed the cot up against the tent wall. An empty cot like his empty marriage. What was the right thing to do? He didn't believe in divorce, but what about annulment, especially when he had been deceived? What would God expect? When he had first invited her to stay tonight, he had been appalled at his own invitation. It was best not to get too close yet.

He saw her shadow hesitate outside the door. Was she going to turn and leave? He stepped forward and pushed up the tent flap. "I'm here. Come on in." He took her small valise and put it on the floor by her cot. She looked like a bird who might take flight at any time. The fading light silhouetted her slim figure and illuminated her hair like a halo. She had certainly acted like an angel of mercy today. The doctor had been very impressed with her.

"Shall we go to mess?" She needed fattening up. A strong wind would carry her to Arizona Territory by itself.

Bessie nodded. "Do you know what we're having?"

"Beans."

Her lips curved upward. "That's all we ever have. Do we ever get vegetables or fruit?"

"You mean like potatoes and apples? Is that what they're called? It's been so long since I've seen one, I'm not sure anymore. I don't think the army knows what they are either." He took her arm and guided her toward the tent opening.

He joked with her during mess and noticed how often other soldiers stopped by to talk to her. She talked easily with them and seemed genuinely interested in each of them. He was surprised to find he was jealous. He wanted those gray eyes to light up at the sight of him like they had earlier today. Was there more to her than he had first thought?

Dusk had begun to fall when they strolled back to his tent. She was obviously nervous, and he was a bit uneasy himself. He needed to keep the fact firmly in mind that she might soon be on her way back to Boston. And he needed to keep his distance so an annulment would be possible.

Jasper shut the flap on the tent and lit the candle on the crate by the opening. He lit another and handed it to Bessie. She smiled her thanks and perched on the edge of her cot. It was too early to go to bed. What were they to do all evening?

She filled in the silence. "Tell me about yourself, Jasper. We hardly know one another."

He seated himself on his cot across from her. "I'm a boring subject."

"You've seen a lot of the world. This is my first time out of Boston."

"You've never been to Texas then."

She shook her head. "Was that where you grew up?"

"There and Ohio. Jessica and I lived in Toledo, Ohio, until our real mother died. I don't remember our father. When we were put in the orphanage, we tried to stay together, but we didn't have any choice. Jessica was adopted by the Dubois family while I was sent West on an orphan train. That was the hardest day of my life. I knew I'd never see my sister again. And I wouldn't have, if it hadn't been for Clay." He smiled, remembering how he felt when he got the telegram from Clay.

"I remember standing on the siding in Abilene while the train blew its horn and pulled away. All my friends were on that train, and it left me behind with a gruff man and a sober woman who said they were my new parents. I was terrified. But the Mendenhalls were great folks. It wasn't their fault they were never able to make me feel like I belonged. They tried, but I could never quit waiting for them to throw me out or scream at me for spilling my milk the way my real mom did."

He hadn't realized he had drifted into reliving the past until Bessie touched his hand. Her soft gray eyes were tender with compassion.

She glanced at her hand on his arm, and a splash of pink stained her cheeks. She left her hand where it was, though. "I'm sorry. You've gone through a lot. But hasn't God been good to reunite you and Jessica?"

She was so right. He laid a hand over hers. "I thank him for it every day. What about you? What was it like growing up for you?"

Her color deepened. She pulled her hand away and looked down. There was some mystery here. What was her real reason for coming out as a wife to someone she had never met? Sure, it was already done when she found out about it, but she could have written and had it annulled or questioned the legality of it. She would have never had to meet him. Why had she?

"What's Lenore really like?" As soon as he asked the question, he wished he could snatch it back.

The light in her eyes died, and she sat back on her cot. "She's a wonderful girl," she said slowly. "Everyone says so. Beautiful, cultured, adventurous. Everything I'm not." She stood and turned her back to him as she stared down at his tiny cache of three books atop his mess chest.

He rose and looked over her shoulder, then turned her to face him. "I didn't mean to hurt you. I wasn't comparing the two of you. I just wondered about the sadness in your eyes. Let's talk about something else."

She gave him a slight smile and picked up a tiny carved buffalo. "This is exquisite. Wherever did you get it?"

"I made it."

"You carved this? Do you have others you've done?"

"Sure." He felt a little strange showing them to her. His hobby of whittling sometimes seemed useless and embarrassing to him. But he carried his knife along wherever he went, and whittling helped calm his mind. No one had ever seemed to think this talent remarkable. With a warm wave of affection for her, he opened

42

his mess chest and pulled out the small gunnysack that held his work.

Her delight in the tiny carved animals washed away the last of his self-consciousness. "This is Lollie, the golden retriever I had as a kid. She died three years ago." He ran his fingers over the smooth surface, then handed it to her.

"Oh, Jasper, look at the devotion on her face." She gave him such a smile of approval, he had to grin. Her joy was contagious. "I brought my paints with me. Once we get settled, I shall have to try to show the beauty of this country." She took his hand and rubbed her fingers over the scars. "I wondered where these nicks and cuts came from."

The touch of her small hand did funny things to his heart. Was that normal? He hadn't been around women much. "Sometimes I get so intent on what I'm doing, the knife gets away from me."

She released his hand, and he felt oddly forlorn. He had liked the feel of her small hand in his. He mentally shook himself and dug into the bag again. "Do you know who this is?"

She looked at the figurine a moment. "Is it Jessica as a child?"

He nodded. "How did you know without the red hair as a flag?"

She stared at it again. "The slant of the eyes and the imperious expression."

He chuckled and she joined him. "She's a lot mellower than she used to be, according to Clay. Jessica admits it too. God has changed her."

"He changes us all." Bessie sighed and put the figurines back in the bag. "Do you ever wonder why he fashioned you as he did?"

"What do you mean?" Was there something about him she didn't like?

"Nothing. Forget it." She yawned and sat on the cot.

All his confidence evaporated. Did she hate red hair?

"I'm really tired. Do you suppose I could go to bed now?"

"Of course." He suddenly realized she had no privacy to get ready for bed. He looked around, then grabbed a blanket. "Let me fix an area for you." He dug some twine out of his mess chest and strung off a section in the corner, then draped the blanket over it. "I've got a couple of things to do before bed. I'll be back in a little while."

She took her valise and started to her privacy corner. Before she slipped the blanket back, she turned to him and smiled. "Thank you for a lovely evening, Jasper. I enjoyed getting to know you better."

He almost sighed with relief. She didn't seem angry with him. What had caused the barrier between them just now? "You're welcome. Call me if you need anything."

"I will."

He left her to get ready for bed and stepped out under the stars. Why had he been so eager to get married anyway? Was it because he'd missed out on having his sister with him for so many years? Did he even know how to be a husband?

With Jasper gone Bessie felt like weeping. Things had gone so well until he mentioned Lenore. Would she live in the shadow of her beautiful sister, even in marriage? Jasper could never have Lenore now. Did he still pine for the spirited girl with whom he had corresponded?

Bessie wasn't as beautiful as Lenore, but that didn't make her own desires less important. She was just quieter about it. With Lenore, everything was done with fanfare and a flurry of activity. Bessie liked to accomplish things quietly in the background.

He had seemed curious when she asked if he ever wondered why God had fashioned him as he did. Was she the only one who ever wondered about that? Why had he chosen to give Lenore all the physical beauty in the family? Did he love her more than Bessie? The Bible called David a man after God's own heart, and David had been handsome and sought after. Did that mean he loved others less? Often Bessie pondered these questions.

She sniffed away her tears, swallowed the lump in the back of her throat, and undressed. She pulled on her flannel, high-necked nightgown and took down her hair. Pushing aside the blanket, she took out her brush and sat on the edge of her cot. One, *two*, *three*. Counting each stroke of the brush, she didn't hear Jasper come in until he cleared his throat.

Her head jerked up, and her mouth went dry at his expression. No man had ever looked at her like that. Could it be that he actually liked the way she looked? She swallowed and stared into his eyes. "I–I'm almost ready for bed." Her fingers felt as though they could barely hang on to the brush.

He cleared his throat again, and his gaze followed the brush as it flowed through her hair. "Could I do that for you?"

It was all Bessie could do to keep her mouth from dropping open. "If–if you like." She handed him the brush and turned so her back was to him. He touched her hair so gently at first, she could barely feel it. "You won't hurt me."

He ran the brush through her hair, his hands following behind the strokes. It felt almost like a caress. Did he mean it as one? The pulse hammered in her throat.

"You have lovely hair." His voice was husky. "Like silk."

If she had tried to answer, she would not have been able to say a word. She closed her eyes and shivered at the sensation of his hands in her hair. She couldn't even remember the last time her mother had brushed her hair. It must have been years ago when she was a child. She tried not to think about what Lenore's hair looked like. Jasper didn't know Lenore's hair was as black as a raven's wing and just as glossy, that Bessie's own waist-length locks were only a pale reflection of her sister's. And Bessie was fiercely glad of that. If he never actually saw Lenore, maybe someday he could grow to love his wife.

He dropped the brush in her lap. "I'd better let you get some sleep."

With reluctance she opened her eyes. The dream was over. Back to reality. He would think back and regret he had touched her when it was Lenore he really wanted. She put the brush back into her valise, then slipped beneath the rough woolen blanket. "Good night, Jasper."

She could sense his gaze on her for several long moments. "Good night, Bessie. Sleep well." He blew out the candle, and she heard him slide into bed. Within a few minutes she heard his breathing deepen. How could he sleep? She didn't think she would be able to sleep at all. The sentry called the time every hour, and the last one she heard was two o'clock.

She awoke to the sound of reveille and the shouts of soldiers packing the column for departure.

"I was about to wake you. We need to pack so I can tear down our tent." Jasper was fully dressed with his hair slicked back. The dim glow of the candle cast shadows on his face.

Bessie sat up groggily and pushed her hair out of her face. That searching expression was on his face again. She flushed self-consciously. "I must look a fright."

"You look lovely. I'm sorry to rush you. I'll be outside when you're ready."

She waited until he closed the flap behind him, then slipped out of the cot. He had called her lovely. Could he really think that?

A battered tin pitcher held the water he had brought in for her. How thoughtful. A flush raced up her cheeks at the dream-like remembrance of his hands in her hair last night. More shouts echoed through the tent wall, and she hurriedly washed and dressed, then pushed the flap aside and stepped outside. Dawn was just beginning to cast rosy fingers across the horizon, and she was chagrined that she had slept so late. What must Jasper think of her?

"Do you want to ride in the ambulance today, or would you like to try the horse again?" The teasing note in Jasper's voice brought the heat to her cheeks again.

"I'd better ride in the ambulance until you have time to teach me to handle a horse."

He grinned. "That's probably a good idea. Maybe we'll have a chance for your first lesson tonight." He touched her arm, then went to help take down the remaining tents.

Her skin tingled where his fingers had been. She rubbed her arm absentmindedly. She sighed and took her valise and hurried to the ambulance. Several of her patients from yesterday were up and gone after a night of rest. She wouldn't get to spend the night in Jasper's tent again.

Doctor Richter fingered his gray handlebar mustache, then waved her over. "Ah, Mrs. Mendenhall, I was wondering if I would have your assistance today. As you can see, our patient load has dwindled overnight."

"How is Private Brindle doing this morning?" Bessie knelt beside the young man who had taken a bullet through the shoulder. He winked at her, and heat burned her face. She wasn't used to such attention.

"Better," he answered at the same time as Doctor Richter.

His fever was down, and his color was better. Bessie gave

him a smile and patted his shoulder before moving on to the next patient.

While she followed the doctor from patient to patient, her thoughts kept drifting to Jasper. What was he doing? Was he thinking of her at all? She shook her head at her thoughts. He was likely thinking about Lenore.

The day stretched out interminably. As evening approached Bessie kept glancing out the back of the covered wagon and watching for Jasper. Would he come to take her riding, or was he already regretting his invitation?

Just before supper mess, he appeared at the back of the wagon. He looked tired, but his face brightened when he saw her. "Would you care to walk with me to supper? Afterward we can go riding." He picked up her valise. "We might as well drop this in our tent on the way."

Our tent. Her heart pounded. *He said* our *tent.* Did he expect them to be together from now on? She smiled at the thought. Perhaps last night had meant something to him after all. She followed him past the huddled tents and campfires. The smoke stung her eyes, but she liked the scent. He tossed her valise into a tent near the center of the encampment, then took her hand. His fingers were warm and comforting. She curled her fingers around his and smiled at him.

After supper they went to the corral, and he picked out a gentle mare for her. He instructed her on mounting and dismounting, using the reins, and saddling the horse. Then he helped her mount. She clung to the pommel and tried not to remember her last disastrous ride. But this time they were both prepared for her inexperience. First Jasper led her on the horse around the encampment. Several soldiers called out encouragement, and Bessie flushed with embarrassment. Did they all know she was a total novice? But the teasing was good-natured, and she soon relaxed.

Then Jasper gave her the reins and walked beside her while she practiced guiding the mare. "You're doing great!" he told her.

Was that pride on his face? She sat taller in the saddle. She wanted Jasper to always look at her with that air of pride and proprietorship.

They stopped at dusk, and Jasper lifted her off the saddle. Bessie's stomach fluttered at the touch of his strong hands on her waist. He held her a few moments longer than necessary, then smiled slightly and released her. As they walked back to the tent, he took her hand.

He tied the flap behind them while she lit the candles, and she felt as though they were a loving married couple settling in for the night. Did he feel anything for her at all? Even if he did, would the memory of Lenore's deception always be between them?

Five

Jasper picked up the envelope and stared at the familiar writing. Bessie's writing. The Bessie he had thought he had known anyway. The real Bessie was back at the tent waiting for him to join her. His mouth dry, he opened Lenore's letter and unfolded the pages inside. At least she signed her real name this time. He leaned against the wagon and quickly scanned the pages, then folded them up and put them in his pocket and strode toward the tent. He wouldn't think about the contents, not now.

He didn't know what to do about the letter's contents. Just reading it brought back his feelings of betrayal. He had been so foolish. Shame burned in his belly and resentment flared against Bessie. Could she really have been innocent of any involvement in Lenore's duplicity? It seemed hard to believe.

Bessie smiled when he entered the tent, but he frowned instead and her smile faltered. "Is something wrong?"

"I need some time to think, Bessie." He took off his hat and raked a hand through his hair. Why did Lenore write to him now? What did she expect from him?

"Some time? What do you mean?"

"I just wonder if this can ever work out. The deceit this began with is too much to overcome. Maybe it would be best if you went back to the ambulance." He wanted to add that any repercussions would be on her head, but he bit back the words. He steeled himself for tears. She deserved a bit of suffering for all she had done.

Her gray eyes filled with tears, and she rose to her feet and stared at him. She started toward the door, then stopped and whirled around to face him, her hands on her slim hips as she glared at him. "I shall do no such thing, Jasper! How can you even ask such a thing? What would the soldiers think if you cast me off after two nights together? It would leave me open to unkind comments and even actions. I am your wife. You may not love me, but I must insist on the same respect you would give your sister or any female under your protection."

His anger flared, but with it came a sense of shame. He gave a stiff nod. "Very well. You may continue to abide in my tent for the time being. When we get to Arizona Territory, we shall discuss what to do with this so-called marriage." He turned and walked out. He would wait until she was asleep before he went back.

❧

Bessie's eyes burned as she watched him go. What had changed? He had been so gentle and sweet today when they were riding. She just didn't understand. Her high hopes had sunk into despair.

Maybe it would be best to let him annul the marriage and just end this struggle. She shook her head. No, she couldn't bear the shame of going back to Boston after being cast off. Out here, no one would think anything about it, but in Boston there would be titters and jokes. She wouldn't be able to hold up her head.

She had been the one left sitting in a chair along the wall at coming-out parties and balls. She had overheard myriad comments from sour dowagers about how she was not the beauty her sister was. Their parents had fussed over Lenore and relegated Bessie to a position more like that of the younger daughter instead of the elder. She had accepted all of these snubs, but she would not sit in the shadows again. Now was the time to stand and fight.

She closed her eyes, then pressed her lips together and straightened her shoulders. Jasper was a decent man, and he was her husband. He might want to find a loophole, but she did not. She would not make it easy for him to set her aside. Her throat tightened with panic, but she had to make it work. What could she do out here with no husband?

Her only hope was in showing him she could be a proper wife, but she had little time to accomplish it. They would be to the new post in another two weeks. She doubted an attorney could be found there, so Jasper would have to write one back East. He would not hear back for some time. Her advantage was the shortage of women in the West. Perhaps that consideration would be enough to slow him down.

She pulled her nightgown on and crawled under the blanket.

After she had cried for a few minutes, she dried her eyes. *Don't be a ninny.* She needed a plan, not tears. But when she finally fell asleep, she was no closer to knowing how to prove to Jasper that he needed her.

⟠

The tension of the last few weeks began to drain Bessie's drive and determination. Jasper avoided her as much as possible, and the times they were together, he was cool and remote. They had no more hair-brushing moments. As the days dragged by she longed for the wagon train to reach Fort Bowie. Maybe in their own home they would be able to find common ground again.

When they were almost to Arizona Territory, their last obstacle was a forty-foot gorge they had to cross by means of a rope-and-board bridge. The gorge fell so deep, Bessie couldn't see the bottom. Another wagon rattled along the planks toward them, but instead of waiting until it passed, her driver lashed his horse and started across too. There might be room for them to pass, but a sense of panic choked her, and she shouted to the driver. "Stop! I'm getting out." She scrambled to the back of the ambulance and pushed back the flap.

The private looked back and shook his head. "I ain't stoppin', missus. Hang tight."

"You either stop, or I'll jump out with it moving. What will my husband do if I'm hurt because you refused to stop?" Most likely he would be glad, but Bessie didn't let herself think about that. She wanted out of this wagon.

Still grumbling, the private shrugged. "Whoa." He pulled on the reins and got down to help her out.

She didn't wait for assistance but scrambled out the back. The bridge swayed in the wind, and she felt sick. She couldn't look over the side, or she would humiliate herself and Jasper.

As if the thought of him had summoned his presence, he rode up. "What's going on? Why have you stopped?"

She answered before the private could. "I will walk across. It's not safe with the other wagon coming."

He looked toward the swaying bridge. "You might be right." He nodded to the private. "Back up and wait until the way is clear. We'd rather get there late than have a disaster."

The soldier shot Bessie a glare, then did as he was told.

A prospector who had been riding with the army detachment muttered an oath and swung his wagon past the ambulance. Jasper shouted at him to wait, but he ignored the warning. His mule trotted toward the approaching wagon. Bessie watched in horror as the prospector came abreast of the other wagon, and the front wheel of one caught the rear wheel of the other. She shuddered at the squeal of metal grating against metal.

The mule reared, and the next moment both the mule and wagon, along with the prospector, vanished over the edge. The mule and the man both screamed a bloodcurdling sound that brought bile to Bessie's throat.

She seized the edge of the ambulance and hung on as her vision blurred and went dark. She mustn't faint. Jasper grabbed her, and she clung to him with all her strength. Other soldiers rushed past them. The pounding of Jasper's heart under her ear calmed her, and she finally pulled away. "I'm fine," she said, wiping her eyes.

"That could have been you. Thank God you stopped the ambulance and got out."

One of the patients poked his head out the back of the ambulance. "You saved our lives, ma'am." His face was pale beneath his grizzled beard, and he stared at her with an expression approaching awe. "You must be pretty close to God."

She smiled faintly. "Not close enough, Private."

Jasper put an arm around her shoulders. "Why don't you ride with me for a while?"

"I'm not sure I can get on the horse." She still felt weak and shaky.

"I'll help you."

Did he actually want to spend time with her? He had been avoiding her for days. "I'll try."

He kept his arm around her as they found the remuda, and he picked out the same mare she had ridden before. He helped her mount, and she felt a bit better with the wind in her face and the warm sun on her arms. After vaulting into the saddle, he took the reins and led her horse across the bridge. She kept her eyes averted when they passed the spot where the prospector had gone over.

"Can we recover his body?"

Jasper shook his head. "Too dangerous."

She fell silent. This was a harsh country where a man could fall to his death and his bones be left for the birds to pick. Did she even want to stay? One look at the man beside her convinced her she did. No matter how hard it was.

On the other side of the bridge, the terrain grew even more desolate. Jasper picked his way through prickly pear cactus and mesquite brush. When they neared a grove of gnarled creosote bushes, she heard a faint sound. "What is that?"

Jasper paused. "I didn't hear anything."

It came again. "There. Did you hear?"

He listened again. "It's the wind."

"I don't think so." She turned her horse's head and proceeded toward the bushes.

"Bessie, we need to move along. It's nothing but the wind."

It sounded like a baby. Impossible. The accident had made her skittish, but she had to know for sure. When she reached the bushes, she slid to the ground. Jasper was impatient, and she sent him a coaxing smile. After a moment he returned the smile and shrugged.

A dark bundle lay beneath the nearest bush. At first she thought it was a rock, but it moved, and she rushed forward. A gaunt Indian woman lay nearly hidden beneath the brush. Was she dead? Bessie touched her and found her cold. Yes, she had passed on, poor woman.

What had moved? She turned to call to Jasper, when she

heard that mewling sound again. Crawling beneath the scrub, she moved the blanket and found a newborn child sucking on her fist.

Bessie gasped, and Jasper was at her side at once.

He took her arm and started to move her out of the way, but she darted forward and picked up the baby. "Oh, poor thing!"

"Is she dead?"

"The mother is. Can you see to a proper burial for her? I need to get this baby to the doctor."

"I'll call some of the men. I should check with our Indian scouts, too, and see if they have any idea who she is or what tribe she's from."

Bessie sent him a grateful smile, then hurried to the ambulance with the baby.

The doctor raised his bushy eyebrows when she rushed into the ambulance with a naked baby in her arms. He took the infant from Bessie and laid her on a cot. He pinched a fold of skin between his fingers. "She's very dehydrated. She likely won't live, Mrs. Mendenhall."

"She *will* live. I'll take care of her."

The doctor shrugged. "What will she eat? We have no nursing woman here."

Bessie thought fast. "The goat. I can feed her goat's milk."

He nodded grudgingly. "Might work if you can rig up some way of getting enough down her."

For the next few days Bessie fought for the life of the tiny Indian girl. She dipped a rag in milk and fed the baby nearly around the clock. Jasper checked in every few hours, and Bessie thought he was getting attached to the tiny baby too. Finally the doctor pronounced the infant out of danger.

What was she going to do with the baby? Bessie fiercely wanted to keep her, but she was almost afraid to ask Jasper. She wrapped the infant in a scrap of blanket and took her to their tent. Perhaps if Jasper became attached to her, he would suggest it.

She felt as though she hadn't been in their tent in days, and she smiled at the curious sense of homecoming. After placing the baby on the cot, she took off her bonnet and washed her face. She'd scarcely taken time for herself since the baby's discovery, but now she took down her hair. Before she could comb it and put it back up, Jasper came in.

A gentle expression came over his features when he saw her. Did he care for her more than he would admit? It was probably just wishful thinking on her part.

"You're back." He glanced toward the cot and frowned. "What are we to do with her? I'm not sure what tribe she's from, but I would suspect Navajo or Apache."

"What do you think we should do?" *Please say we can keep her.* Her heart pounded as she waited for his answer.

His frown deepened. "It would be hard, if not impossible, to find her family. I don't know if there are any orphanages in Phoenix or Tucson. I suppose we could try to locate one."

Her eyes blurred with tears. She couldn't give the baby up. She tried to speak, but she could not get any words out past the lump in her throat. Bessie kept her head down, but Jasper put his fingertips on her chin and lifted her face.

"You want to keep her, don't you?"

"Yes," she whispered.

"What if we end this marriage? Will you take her back to Boston? Will people there accept her?"

His words were gentle, but she sensed the steely purpose behind them. He still wanted to get rid of her. Tears flooded her eyes again, and she jerked her chin away. He didn't need to gloat over her pain. She turned her back to him. "Can't we worry about that if and when it happens?"

He sighed. "You'll get so attached to her, it will be impossible to give her up."

"I already am." She identified with the baby, for she had often felt like an unwanted waif herself. She wanted the child to feel the love and acceptance she had craved all her life.

Jasper was silent, and she risked a glance at him from under her lashes. He was still frowning, and her heart sank.

"Very well. But don't blame me when you have to find her another adoptive family when you go back to Boston."

She felt a mixture of pain and joy at his words. He still intended to send her back to Boston, but at least she would have the baby. She turned and focused the full force of her smile on him. He blinked and looked away.

"She needs a name," she said.

"What do you have in mind?"

"Ruth. She followed Naomi away from her own people the way this baby will follow us from her tribe."

Jasper nodded. "Good choice of name, but we may regret this decision."

"I won't."

He sighed. "I guess I'd better get started on a cradle for her. She'll need to have somewhere to sleep." He pushed open the flap and went outside.

Bessie sank onto the floor and stared at little Ruth in relief. "Mama will take care of you, sweetheart. I won't let anyone hurt you." She took the baby's hand, and the tiny fingers closed around hers. Now the stakes for preserving the marriage were higher. She couldn't let Ruth down.

By evening Jasper had knocked together a cradle for Ruth. He had even carved bunnies and her name on the headboard. Bessie hugged him when he brought it in. He looked like a little boy who had brought his mother a fistful of flowers, pleased and embarrassed at the same time. Ruth seemed to know it belonged to her, because once in the cradle, she put her thumb in her mouth and went to sleep almost immediately.

The weather turned unbearably hot as they plunged deeper into the heart of Arizona Territory. Bessie and the baby were both lethargic from the heat. They stopped for a day in Phoenix, a small settlement of nearly fifty people. Bessie saw several other women and yearned to spend some time with them, but the army wagons moved forward before she could get the courage to approach them. The trail led south through rocky outcroppings and saguaro cactus.

"Fort Bowie ahead!" the scout at the head of the column shouted.

Bessie made sure Ruth was asleep in her cradle in the ambulance, and then she climbed out. She scanned the horizon for a look at her new home. All she saw was a small cluster of ramshackle adobe buildings surrounded by an adobe wall. Her heart sank. It was even worse than she had imagined.

Jasper grinned at her from near the front of the column. She could see his excitement even from a distance. She smiled back feebly. If he would smile at her like that every day, it would be adequate compensation for what she would have to endure.

The gates swung open, and the wagons rolled into the fort. Bessie jumped onto the ambulance as it came past and climbed back inside. When the wagon finally stopped, she picked Ruth up and went to see where they would live. She didn't know if she was ready to see it, but there was no choice. They were here, and they must make the best of it.

Bessie stared in dismay. There were nearly as many wagons as there were buildings. The windows of most of the buildings were open holes, and many of the roofs were gone. Dust and sand made a dismal backdrop to the tiny fort. She clutched Ruth and gazed around in numb horror.

Jasper directed the soldiers as they unpacked and stowed the supplies they had brought. She shuddered and climbed back inside the ambulance. She could wait to see their quarters. They were likely much worse than the wagon.

It was nearly dusk when Jasper finally came for them. Dust had crept into the lines of exhaustion around his mouth and nose. His uniform was covered with a fine coating of dust and sand too. Poor man. She would not complain and make it worse.

"Ready? I haven't had a chance to check out our quarters, but I'm heading there now. Most of the buildings will need to be rebuilt, but at least our place has a roof."

Bessie picked Ruth up from her cradle, and Jasper lifted Bessie's valise. He led her across the dusty ground to a small adobe building on the south end. There was no stoop and sand covered the threshold.

Jasper pushed the door open and stepped inside. Bessie followed him eagerly. As her eyes adjusted to the dim interior, she let her gaze travel around the room. Their quarters consisted of three rooms. A tiny parlor led into a minuscule kitchen. Off the kitchen was a tiny bedroom. There was no furniture, and thick dust covered the rough plank floor. Her heart sank at the filthy condition of the home.

"We can't sleep here tonight." Dismay filled Jasper's voice.

Bessie mustered every ounce of courage she possessed. "If you can find me a broom and some cleaning supplies, I'll see what I can do."

He stared at her. "You'll clean it yourself?"

"It's a typical chore for a wife."

Admiration shone on his face as he smiled at her. "I'll be back with your supplies."

When he was gone, she wanted to sink to the floor and weep. For all her brave words, she didn't know how she could clean this in a week, let alone an hour. But she had to try. This was her first real opportunity to demonstrate to Jasper just what kind of wife she could be. Her entire future and that of Ruth's hung in the balance.

Six

When Jasper had been told the troops would rebuild the fort, he had expected to find more to work with than what was available. Speed was of the utmost importance. Cochise had begun a reign of terror along the Butterfield Trail nearly two years ago, and the nation had endured it as long as it intended. The army's job was to provide protection to travelers and homesteaders in the area, but until they had somewhere to stay, that would have to wait. He regretted bringing Bessie and Ruth here. The crumbling stockade was little protection against the fearsome Apache tribe.

He didn't know what to tell Bessie. He still couldn't believe the army had sent them all this way to rebuild the fort but had sent no lye or soap. If he could just find a broom, Bessie might be able to make a beginning, but there were none. He found a stick and whittled it down to a semismooth shape. Then he attached some brush to the end with twine. It would have to do.

When he returned to the house, Bessie had found an empty crate. She had dragged it to the center of the room and sat on it with Ruth in her arms. Jasper felt a pang of regret they weren't the happy family they appeared, but he pushed the thought away. He didn't have time to think about that now. There was too much work to do.

Bessie sent him a gentle smile. "What is that? It looks like a porcupine on a stick."

He grinned. "I knew my broom-making skills left much to be desired, but I thought you'd at least recognize it."

Her mouth dropped open, but she recovered quickly. "You made me a broom? Were the rest gone?" She stood, handed the baby to him, and took the broom. "Can you watch her? It would probably be best to take her out of here while I'm sweeping so she doesn't breathe the dust."

The baby's bottom was soggy, and he grimaced. "She's wet."

"Clean clothes are in the ambulance. I'll go get them." She dropped the broom and started toward the door.

"No, no. I'll do it. It can't be that hard."

She smiled and picked up the broom again. Dust flew, and he coughed and backed away. Ruth's wet bottom began to soak through his coat, and he shuddered. He had already offered, though, so holding the baby at arm's length, he hurried to the ambulance.

He laid the baby on the seat in the wagon and rummaged through Bessie's small chest until he found a square of soft cloth he assumed was a diaper. Gingerly, he unwrapped the baby's blanket and grimaced. He unpinned the wet diaper and dragged it from under her bottom. He wiped his hand hastily on his pant leg, then slid the clean diaper under the baby. How did this thing connect? After several tries, he managed to get it hooked together, but the diaper drooped.

He found a dry blanket scrap. Bessie had evidently cut a blanket into squares for Ruth. He respected her resourcefulness. What would have become of Ruth if Bessie had not been part of their detachment?

The baby would be dead in the desert like her mother. Bessie was the one who heard the infant's cries. Did it take a woman to hear a baby's weak wails? If he had even heard it, he would have dismissed the sound as a bird or some other kind of animal. Bessie's curiosity had saved this little life.

He stared into the baby's innocent dark eyes. She stared back and gave him a slow, small smile that tugged at his heartstrings. He waggled a finger at her, and she wrapped her tiny fingers around it. She was going to be a charmer, all right. When he wrapped her in the blanket, she popped her thumb in her mouth and promptly fell asleep. Weren't babies supposed to cry more? She hadn't let out a peep while he cared for her, and she didn't seem to mind a droopy diaper at all.

Such a cute baby with a thick head of black hair and smooth, soft skin. He nestled her against his chest and walked across the dusty parade ground to the quartermaster tent, where he arranged for cots and kitchen supplies. By the time he concluded his business and went back across the barren yard, nearly an hour and a half had passed. He wasn't expecting much improvement in their quarters, since Bessie didn't have anything to work with. They would have to stay in a tent tonight.

Pushing open the door, he stopped in amazement. Instead of sand and dirt crunching beneath his feet, the rough floor-boards were clean and scrubbed. It looked like they had even been mopped, which meant Bessie would have had to do that on her hands and knees. The dirty fireplace hearth had been swept and new logs laid. Cobwebs no longer festooned the corners of the ceilings, and the rooms even smelled cleaner. How did she do it? Suddenly, changing the diaper didn't seem to be something worth bragging about.

He walked through the parlor and the kitchen until he found Bessie in the tiny bedroom. She was on her hands and knees, scrubbing the floors with what looked like wet sand. A little pile of sand was heaped about four feet from her where she had swept it up. Dark smudges of dirt marred the silky-white perfection of her skin, and Jasper thought she looked tired. No wonder. She had worked the entire time he was gone.

Unnoticed, he stood observing her for a few minutes. Her hair covered with a kerchief, she knelt to her task, while her slim shoul-ders flexed with the force of her scrubbing. When she stopped to push a stray strand of hair out of her eyes, she saw him standing in the doorway. Her eyes widened, and she got to her feet. Hurrying to his side, she held out her arms for the baby.

Jasper handed over Ruth. "This place looks splendid. I have

some cots on their way. If you can keep the baby now, I'll knock together some kind of kitchen table and benches."

"Did you bring her cradle?" The blanket fell open as she took the infant, and Ruth's sagging diaper was exposed. Bessie looked startled, then smiled. "I see you managed to get her changed."

"It's not as easy as it looks," he admitted gruffly. "The cradle is on its way with the rest of our things." He put his hand on her shoulder. "You worked hard here. Thank you."

Her expression of surprise and delight shamed him. He didn't want her to think he was an ogre who didn't appreciate her efforts. Startled at how much he wanted her good opinion, he backed away. "You've done enough for tonight. At least the bugs and sand are gone."

"What about the open windows? I'd feel better if they were covered with something. Would the quartermaster have some thin cloth we could tack up? I don't want anything heavy enough to block out the breeze, just the bugs."

"I'll see what I can find. There are only three windows, so it won't take a lot of fabric. It's almost dark, though. It may have to wait until morning. Can you bear it for one night?"

"Of course. We just need to make sure Ruth isn't bitten by a spider or a scorpion. I'll have to be vigilant."

"We'll be careful." He was surprised to find her frail appearance hid a competent woman.

The quartermaster had already closed shop when he walked back across the parade ground. They would have to deal with the open windows tonight. Looking out over the dark hills, he shivered. Cochise was out there, and they had little protection here. He had a responsibility to Bessie and Ruth now. Bugs were the least of their worries.

☙

Bessie rocked Ruth in her arms and crooned to her. She was exhausted, but the admiration on Jasper's face had been worth all her hard work. Was he beginning to see her differently? It certainly seemed so, but she was almost afraid to hope. Maybe it was her own wishful thinking.

Two privates had brought their belongings, but the three small rooms still looked bare. Could this ever be a home? She had to try, but it seemed an impossible task. With a sigh, she wearily put the baby into her cradle and went to make up the cots. The privates had placed two in the tiny bedroom and pushed them together. That would never do. In fact, she would ask Jasper to sleep in the parlor while she and Ruth took the bedroom. She made the beds and began to unpack the crates and barrels.

"I thought you'd be in bed by now."

She jumped at the sound of Jasper's voice. "I was just trying to put the last of our things away."

He took the crate lid from her hand. "You're done for the day."

The way he was staring at her brought the blood pounding to her cheeks.

He stroked her cheek. "You're tired. I'll take the cot in the parlor. You and Ruth can have the bedroom."

She appreciated his perception. She didn't even need to ask him. "Are you sure you'll be all right out here? This room has the biggest window."

"You are more worried about the windows than I am." He chuckled. "I've slept outside without even a tent over my head more times than I can count."

She smiled. "Very well. Good night."

He didn't answer but continued to stare at her as though he had never seen her before. Did she have a smudge on her nose? She didn't know whether to walk away or stay. Her heart pounded and her mouth went dry.

From the bedroom came an angry wail. "The baby," she whispered. "I must tend to her."

"Yes," he said, but he touched her cheek again, and she couldn't move.

He finally dropped his hand. "She sounds outraged."

"She's probably hungry again. She eats better since we got the bottle in Phoenix, but she's making up for lost time now."

He nodded. "See you tomorrow."

She took a calming breath and hurried to the kitchen. She removed the bottle of milk from the cooling water bucket, then prepared Ruth's meal. Bessie felt Jasper's gaze on her, and the knowledge made her curiously clumsy. She breathed a sigh of relief when she was finally able to close the bedroom door behind her and focus on the baby. She didn't know what to think. What had happened? Perhaps he was simply grateful for the cleaning she had done.

She fed the baby, and then she took her Bible from the makeshift table beside the cot. She needed all the wisdom she could get on how to deal with this situation. Was she feeling love for Jasper? She just didn't know, but she decided to spend every night finding out what God had to say about love.

⁂

The sun beat through the tiny window and awakened Bessie. She sat up groggily. When she saw how bright it was, she slid to the floor and grabbed her dress. She should have been up hours ago. Why hadn't Ruth cried and awakened her? When she looked into the cradle, she found it empty. She gasped, then smiled slowly. Jasper must have taken her.

When she had finished her ablutions, she hurried into the kitchen. Jasper sat at a rough plank table on a crude wooden bench. Ruth was in his arms, sucking greedily at the bottle. Bessie felt a pang at the homey picture. Would they ever be the happy family she longed for?

She cleared her throat, and Jasper looked up.

"Good morning, sleepyhead. I see you finally decided to join us." His blue eyes were warm.

"Why didn't you wake me?" She stepped farther into the room.

"When this little mite's complaining didn't do the trick, I decided you must need the sleep." He pulled the bottle out of Ruth's mouth and stood. "You can play mommy. I need to get back to work."

"I'm sorry I slept so late." Was he angry with her?

But he smiled and touched her cheek like he did the night before. "I'll try to be back for lunch."

⟋

The next few days flew by. Bessie cared for the baby while trying to make a home in the ramshackle quarters. At times it seemed a losing battle. Dust blew under the door and through the cloth at the windows almost as fast as she could clean it up. Around the fort the men were trying to rebuild the stockade as quickly as possible. Cochise was to the south of the fort, but no one knew when he would be back up this way. Most of the men still slept in tents, but they would soon be under roofs.

The soldiers hired Mexicans and friendly Indians who showed them how to mix adobe and make bricks. One of the Indians, a young brave about twenty-five, was fascinated with Bessie and Ruth. Jasper kept an eye on him, but he was harmless and curious.

Within a week Fort Bowie began to look like a very different place. Jasper organized groups to roof the buildings once the stockade was repaired and they were in a safer position. Bessie worried about him. He often came home looking tired and dirty.

"Those curtains look so sweet and homey," he told her when

she finally got them finished and up on the windows. "Even Major Daniels remarked on it. He's thinking about sending for his wife since you're here."

Bessie felt a sense of jubilation. Was he beginning to think of them as a family? Would he ever look at her with that special look in his eyes he had that night on the trail? She was beginning to wonder if she had imagined it all.

"What's for supper?"

She suppressed a smile at the mirth on his face. So far they had eaten at mess every night, but she needed to get started on learning to cook. She dreaded letting Jasper know she wasn't joking when she said she didn't know how. Although she had brought her grandmother's cookbook with her, some of the directions seemed incomprehensible to her. If another woman came to the fort, Bessie could talk to her about cooking and other concerns.

Sometimes she felt lonely surrounded by men, even though the soldiers were kind and considerate. One private, Rooster Wheeler, a grizzled, red-haired man who reminded her of a banty rooster, especially looked after her.

"Probably beans again," she said.

"Nope." He rummaged in the gunnysack he had laid on the table and produced a small package. "Rooster bagged an antelope this morning. He gave me this roast for 'the little woman,' as he called you." Jasper's lips grew into a huge grin, and he handed her the meat. "You do know how to cook it, don't you?"

"Is there anything to go with it?" What was she going to do?

She had no idea how to cook this hunk of meat, but she couldn't face the humiliation of telling Jasper. He was beginning to think she was competent as a wife. Would Rooster know how to cook it? He caught the antelope, after all.

Jasper produced two wrinkled potatoes filled with eyes. "These were worth their weight in gold, but I gave Corporal Myers the scouting assignment he wanted, so I got them. I also snagged some canned peaches. We shall feast like kings tonight."

She turned away to care for the baby so Jasper couldn't see her face. How hard could it be to cook this roast, anyway? Toss it in a pot with some water and these potatoes and it could be a kind of stew. That sounded good. Her mouth watered at the thought of real meat. Beans grew tiresome after weeks of eating little else. She would consult her cookbook and see what it suggested. At least she could read.

Seven

Jasper reread the letter and frowned. He didn't know whether to be happy or mad. He would have to discuss this with Bessie tonight. The thought of his wife brought a smile to his face. Supper should be ready by now. Would she have fixed a stew with the meat or just roasted it? Thinking of the possibilities made his mouth water. He bounded across the parade ground as he hurried home.

The curtains blew in the hot desert wind as he approached their quarters. The adobe looked clean and scrubbed. He had caught Bessie brushing the debris from the walls of the house the other day. Barely five feet tall, she was standing on one of the benches he had made for the kitchen, and he grinned at the picture she made. The soldiers called her "Angel." He had asked Rooster where the nickname came from, and the old soldier had said she was their angel of mercy. She was always there to listen to a problem or to pull out a splinter. It made Jasper see her in a whole new light. Physically, she was tiny, but her spirit was mighty.

He could smell supper cooking through the open window,

and his grin widened. Stew and fresh-baked bread. He threw open the door and found his way to the kitchen. Bessie stood over the woodstove stirring the pot. She tasted the stew and grimaced.

"Something wrong? It sure smells good."

She made a slow turn. "I guess it's ready."

She didn't seem very enthusiastic. Maybe she wasn't hungry. He took off his hat and poured water into the pitcher to wash his hands. "Ruthie sleeping?"

"She should be waking anytime."

"I reckon we should eat before she does. Then you won't have to be hopping up and down." He dried his hands and sat on the bench expectantly.

Bessie took a cup and ladled stew into the two waiting bowls. She set them on the table, then turned back to the stove. "The biscuits should be done too. I'll get them." She took a cloth, then pulled the biscuits from the oven and put them on the table.

Jasper's mouth watered just looking at them. They were golden brown and looked delicious.

"Thomas was overseeing supplies today. I talked him out of some jam for the biscuits." She sat on the other bench and folded her hands while Jasper said grace.

He picked up his spoon. He couldn't wait to eat something other than the usual mess slop. He took a big spoonful of stew and shoveled it into his mouth. It was so hot it was hard to really taste it for a minute, but then the gamy flavor hit his taste buds. He shot his gaze to Bessie. Her eyes down, she chewed slowly.

The expression on her face looked as though she were in pain. He swallowed and reached for a biscuit. That ought to kill the gamy flavor.

After ladling jam onto a biscuit, he bit into it with appreciation, then spit it back out. "What did you make these out of?" he asked before he could stop the words. "They taste salty."

She frowned and took a biscuit. "I just followed the directions." She broke off a piece of biscuit and put it in her mouth. Shuddering, she discreetly spit it back out. She folded her hands in her lap again and bent her head. "I don't understand it," she murmured.

Jasper got up and studied the ingredients she had on the stove. "How much saleratus did you use? Sour milk and molasses usually work better."

Her eyes filled with tears. "I didn't have any molasses, so I just guessed. I used too much?"

He felt sorry for her. She had tried so hard. He would just eat the stew and not say anything until later about the spices she should have used. There was no reason to make her feel any worse. "You'll learn." He put a hand on her shoulder. "It's better than mess hall food." He sat down and quickly ate the stew.

She took another bite of the stew and burst into sobs. "It's terrible!" She threw down her spoon with a clatter and buried her face in her hands. "I so wanted to impress you," she wailed.

He knelt beside her. "Don't cry. It's no big deal. It's my fault. I should have showed you how to do it. Antelope is tricky. There are special herbs you can use to take the gamy flavor out." He stroked her hair. Her tears made him feel helpless. He pulled her to his chest. "Shh. It's all right."

She'd been a rock through this, showing him a true helpmeet's spirit. Growing up at the Mendenhall's, he hadn't understood how much he craved a real home and family. They'd treated him well, but he'd always been conscious of some lack.

Her sobs stilled, and her hand crept up his chest and nestled at his neck. A wave of protective tenderness swept over him, and he suddenly realized how much he liked the feel of her in his arms. She was small and compact and fit neatly against him—like she belonged.

When she lifted her head, he stared into her gray eyes. Was that fear in them? He cupped her cheek. After a moment she closed her eyes, and he kissed her. The shock of her soft lips against his was like the kick of a mule.

He didn't want it to end, but she finally pulled away from him. Uncertainty filled her face, and she had good reason. Neither one of them knew where they stood.

Tears pooled in her eyes again, and he wanted to ask her why, but he was afraid to speak, afraid of seeing that soft expression fade from her face. Did she love him? Did he love her? He enjoyed the kiss, but was that love? What was love, really? He didn't think he even knew.

From the bedroom they heard Ruth's cry. "She's hungry," Bessie whispered. "I must feed her."

"All right. When she's settled again, I wish to speak with you.

There is something we must discuss." The letter burned in his pocket, and he felt like a traitor knowing what he had to say to her.

He released her, and she got slowly to her feet, then hurried to the bedroom. The frightened expression was back on her face, and there was reason for it this time.

Ruth's cries soon stilled as she sucked eagerly at the bottle. What was it Bessie had seen in Jasper's eyes? She was afraid she didn't want to know what he wanted to talk about. Was he going to send her home now? She couldn't go, she just couldn't. She loved her baby, and she was starting to love Jasper as well. She hadn't wanted to lose her heart until she knew it was safe, but she had been helpless to prevent it.

She sniffled and rubbed her eyes. Well, if that's what he wanted, she wouldn't agree. She would stay and fight if she had to.

Ruth's eyelids soon drooped again, and Bessie put her back into her cradle. Before she went to the parlor, she peered into the little handheld mirror on the nightstand and smoothed her hair. Her eyes looked fearful. She pinched a little color into her cheeks and bit her lips. Straightening her shoulders, she marched into the parlor.

Jasper sprang to his feet when she entered the room. He patted his coat pocket as if to check that something was there, then raked a hand through his red hair. "Sit down, Bessie." He indicated the cot that served as their sofa.

She sat gingerly on the edge of the cot and looked up at him expectantly. Her heart pounded.

He put his hand in his pocket and drew out a letter. "I hadn't mentioned it yet, but I wrote to an attorney in California about our situation. I received his answer today." He avoided her eyes as he pulled the letter out of its envelope and opened it.

She clenched her fists in the folds of her dress. "Why didn't you talk to me about it first? You didn't give me a chance to say anything."

"What is there to say? We needed to find out where we stand in this marriage."

"Very well." She forced herself to sit back and look at him as though she didn't care, when inside she felt as though her heart were literally breaking.

Jasper leaned against the fireplace. "He says that I signed the papers and married myself to Bessie Randall no matter who she was. The fact that she wasn't the person I thought was Bessie didn't matter. You, however, were not involved on your end until it was done. If anyone has grounds for an annulment, it would be you. So if we are to set aside this marriage, you will have to be the one who does it."

"Then it will not be done, because I will not. When I came out here, it was to be your wife. I have not changed my opinion on that because of your disappointment in me."

"I did not say I was disappointed." Jasper finally met her gaze. He sighed and looked away. "I didn't say I wanted you to set it aside. I just wanted you to know you had that option."

"It is no option. Marriage is sacred before God. I would not break my vow."

"That's just the issue, Bessie. It was not your vow, it was Lenore's. Why do you feel you must honor your sister's deception?"

In spite of his assertion that he just wanted her to know she could set the marriage aside if she so desired, had he really thought she would do so?

She couldn't answer his question. She couldn't look into his blue eyes and tell him she loved him, not when he did not love her. In her heart she knew he didn't. But he might one day. Someday he might even give her a ring to wear that showed she belonged to him. She could always hope. She stood and walked to the window.

He sighed. "I would like us to begin to make some progress toward a real marriage, Bessie. Would you be agreeable to studying what God says about love and marriage? I don't feel I really know what love is or how to love you as a husband should love his wife." His voice was tentative. "My adoptive family didn't hold much with religion, but I went to church with a neighbor. I never saw them show much affection to each other either, and theirs was not a marriage I would want for us. I'm not sure I know how to be a good husband, but I want to learn."

It was such an unexpected request that Bessie froze where she was. He wanted to learn to love her. That realization filled her with joy. Perhaps one day she would see genuine love in his face. "That would be lovely." For just a moment she allowed herself to hope.

He picked up the Bible from the top of his mess chest, then sat on the cot and patted the spot beside him. "Sit with me."

She settled in next to him, and he opened the Bible. "May I?"

She found her voice. "Of course." She was afraid to say more, afraid her heart would betray her.

"I asked Clay once what Scripture a husband and wife should read together. He suggested 1 Corinthians 13 to discover what love really is. He told me to beware of thinking love was just a feeling. Shall I begin?"

"Please do."

"Clay said to remember the word *charity* means love." He began to read. The words poured into her heart. She had never heard these words quite like this. Had she ever loved someone this unselfishly? Could she learn to love Jasper like this? It was a bit daunting.

"'Charity suffereth long, and is kind; charity envieth not; charity vaunteth not itself, is not puffed up, Doth not behave itself unseemly, seeketh not her own, is not easily provoked, thinketh no evil.'"

Jasper closed the Bible. "Let's pray." He took Bessie's hand. "Lord, we ask you to show us how to love one another as you would have a husband and wife love. Give us grace and patience and bind our hearts together as one. In Jesus' name, amen."

Tears pooled in Bessie's eyes when she raised her head. His prayer had seemed so heartfelt. Did he really intend to try? She wasn't a beauty, she couldn't cook a decent meal, and she wasn't anything special. Perhaps she could love him enough to make up for those deficiencies.

He smiled at her. "God has given us a pretty big list. I think we should just work on one characteristic at a time. After that meal, long-suffering will be my first goal."

She stared at him, then slowly began to smile as his words penetrated. "At least you got to eat it in the privacy of your own home. And what about the rest of that sentence?" She opened the Bible to Corinthians. "To paraphrase, love suffers long and is kind. How about a little kindness? You could eat those biscuits anyway."

"I'm not that kind," he told her with a grin. "But a stray dog came into the fort today. He would probably consider it a kindness to eat them."

She burst into delighted laughter. "You get the dog, and I'll get the biscuits."

She couldn't believe the difference in their relationship over the next few days. Jasper went out of his way to do small things for her. They spent the evenings reading together from the Bible or the small stash of books she had brought West with her, or they discussed dreams and goals. She discovered Jasper wanted to open a general store in a small town when he was out of the army, and she confessed to him how much she had always wanted a sewing machine. She even got out her paints and tried her hand at a painting of their little abode, then hung it on one small wall.

He sometimes kissed her before she went to the tiny bedroom with Ruth, and she wondered when he would begin to demand his husbandly rights. She so longed to hear him say he loved her, but he never did. Perhaps he never would. If not, she must learn to deal with that fact. They could raise a family on mutual respect and consideration. She wanted a family, a large family. Much as she loved Lenore, she had always regretted having only one sibling.

They were trapped inside one day while a sandstorm blew through. The wind howled and blew sand through every crack and crevice, but they spent the time playing checkers on a battered board with painted rocks Jasper had scrounged. Bessie loved the time together and was almost glad for the storm.

When he went off on patrol the next day, Bessie knew she had her work cut out for her. A thick layer of sand covered everything, even their clothes. After sweeping and dusting, she asked one of the privates to haul her some water for washing. The supply train had come with cleaning supplies, and she was ready to give the house a good cleaning. She filled the tub with soap and water, took down the scrub board from the kitchen wall, rolled up her sleeves, and got to work.

Jasper had left his mess chest open, so she decided to clean everything in it too. She was almost to the bottom of the chest when she found a letter with familiar flamboyant penmanship. Lenore's.

Her throat constricted. Kneeling on the hard wooden floor with the letter in her hand, Bessie's chest felt heavy as though she couldn't breathe. She wanted to crumple the letter into a ball and toss it into the stove.

When had Jasper gotten this letter? Why hadn't he told her he was still corresponding with Lenore? And Lenore. How could she write to her sister's husband behind her back?

The sting of betrayal brought tears of pain and rage to her eyes.

She had known her sister was selfish, but how could she do something like this? Had Lenore's relationship soured with Richard, so she thought to resume her long-distance romance with Jasper? He was a married man now. He was Bessie's husband, not Lenore's.

Bessie had thought things were going so well, but now she discovered he had kept this secret. Her hands shook, and she put the letter down as though it might bite her. She wouldn't read it. She couldn't. She couldn't bear to see words of endearment. Jasper would be home soon, but she didn't want to see him. How could she hide her feelings? But hide them she must.

He must not have the satisfaction of knowing she loved him.

She had never known she could feel such jealousy and anger. How could she face him? He would surely read the pain in her eyes.

She buried the letter in the bottom of the mess chest and piled the rest of Jasper's things on top. Closing the lid, she got to her feet as though she were an old woman. She felt old and used and hurt.

Taking a deep breath, she leaned her forehead against the wall, then straightened her shoulders and forced back tears. She would weather this somehow. She still had Ruth, even if her husband's heart would never be hers.

The baby wailed, and she hurried to care for her. She felt like wailing herself, but she was an adult and her responsibilities waited for her. She wished she could just sit in the middle of the floor and weep until she had no more tears.

Eight

Ruth was crying when Jasper got home. He felt irritable and out of sorts, and a crying baby did nothing to ease his mood. Bessie had been acting oddly for the past week too. He had tried to get her to tell him what was wrong, but she refused to answer him. He had enjoyed coming home to a smiling wife, but this solemn little wife with the stiff back disconcerted him. She still did everything she had done before. The house was spotless with supper on the table when he arrived, but he missed the light in her eyes when she saw him and her ready smile. He had to find out what was wrong.

He picked Ruth up and walked through the kitchen, looking for Bessie. Supper was cooking. It smelled like beans and corn bread, and his stomach rumbled. He finally found her just outside the back door with a pile of wood in her arms.

"Why didn't you wait until I got home? Ruthie was awake and crying."

"I just left her a moment. Rooster brought the wood right up to the back of our quarters. She couldn't have been crying long."

He held the door open while she carried the wood in. He

would have done it for her, but he could tell by her expression it would be best not to offer. She dropped the wood in the box by the stove, then she rinsed her hands in the bowl of water on the dry sink. Holding her arms out for the baby, she didn't meet his gaze.

He sighed and handed Ruth over to her. How was a man supposed to know how he had transgressed with a woman? What man understood women? He wished Clay and Jessica were here. Clay had plenty of experience in dealing with a temperamental woman.

"I'm going to be gone for three or four days," he told her. "I've been assigned patrol duty. Word is Cochise is headed this way. He attacked a wagon train over by Lordsburg, then killed a settler and his family near San Simon."

Her head jerked up, and he could read the fear in her eyes. He felt a sense of relief. Whatever was eating her, at least she still cared about his safety. "I'll be fine." He gave her a smile, and she returned it tentatively.

"The officers are hosting a party at their quarters tonight. You want to go?"

She hesitated, then nodded. "These four walls get tiresome. I wish I could plant a garden, but headquarters did not send any seeds."

"What kind of garden? Vegetables or flowers?"

"Both, really."

"It would be difficult. We would have to haul water."

"I know, but the acequia isn't far."

"It would take more water than you realize."

"A small garden wouldn't take that much."

He smiled and went to the parlor, glad he could surprise her. When he opened his mess chest, he sensed her stiffen. Puzzled, he glanced at her. What was eating at her? Rummaging through his chest, he found a box in the very bottom and pulled it out. "Jessica sent these with me. I had forgotten about them until now."

She gave a cry of delight at the seed packets in his hand. "Bless you!" She snatched the packets from him and riffled through them. "Carrots, green beans, beets, even a packet of flower seeds." She stood on her tiptoes and kissed his chin. "Thank you, Jasper. I'll get started tomorrow."

"Wait until I can help you. The ground will be hard as brick. I doubt you can break it up by yourself." Her enthusiasm pleased him. He wanted things back the way they were. Even their Bible reading at night was tense. He hoped she would get over whatever was bothering her by the time he came back in a few days.

❧

Bessie pushed on the shovel with all her might, but she didn't have the strength to shove more than the tip into the ground. She sighed at her own ineptitude. If she couldn't do something as simple as turning over sod, how could she ever prove to Jasper she was a better wife than Lenore ever could have been for him?

She didn't want to wait to plant the garden until Jasper came home. She needed something to occupy her time now. If she had too much spare time, her mind went round and round her problems. Thoughts of her husband's betrayal were just under the surface of her mind, like an itch that needed to be scratched. The more she tried to ignore it, the more it nagged at her. Would she ever be able to erase the memory of her sister's bold writing on the envelope of that letter?

"Missus, you ought not to be doin' this by yourself. I'm off duty now. Yer husband would have my hide if he knew I'd let you dig this here dirt." Rooster plucked the shovel from her hands and shooed her out of the way. He jammed the shovel to its hilt into the dirt and turned it over.

He might look like a scrawny banty rooster, but he was stronger than he looked. She backed away to where Ruth lay under a blanket canopy and watched. Rooster made it look so easy.

A strange rattling noise made her look down. She froze. A snake! Its coils glistened in the sunshine, its flat, triangular-shaped head low to its body. She tried to call out to Rooster, but before she could get a sound past her tight throat, it struck. Its fangs sank into her leg and she screamed.

Before she fainted, she heard Rooster shout, then the ground rose to meet her.

"Ruthie." Bessie tried to raise her head. Where was she, and where was the baby? Her right leg throbbed and burned, and she felt light-headed and weak.

"Lie still, missus. You been bit." Rooster's voice seemed far away.

"My baby."

"I got the little one right here. She's fine. You gotta lie still."

Gentle hands pushed her down. She gasped, struggling to breathe. A rattlesnake. It had bitten her. She shuddered as nausea washed over her. Rooster held a pail while she vomited.

He muttered clucking noises and patted her shoulder awkwardly when she began to cry. "You'll be all right. I done sucked out the poison."

She turned her head, seeking for sight of the baby. When she saw her sleeping in the cradle, she closed her eyes and slept too. She awakened off and on and cried out for water, for Jasper or for Ruth, but Rooster was always there to hold the pail or give her a drink. Once she thought she saw Lenore sitting on the edge of the bed, but she told her to go away. She had already spoiled things enough. Bessie didn't want her there.

❧

Jasper drooped tiredly in the saddle. How were Bessie and Ruth getting along without him? Maybe Bessie was glad to have him out of the way.

Twenty-three men rode with him. So far they had seen no Apaches, only a few friendly Navajo who had strayed off their reservation. Jasper was beginning to wonder if their information was correct. Cochise might have headed back into the Dragoon Mountains. He had been a formidable foe, striking small parties and settlers, then fading back to his hideaway in the mountains, but now that the fort was operational again, he would be even more cautious. Most tribes avoided the white man's forts and the "guns that shoot twice," as they called the army's howitzers.

Jasper came over the rise of a mesa and signaled the men to stop. He took the spyglass and searched the countryside. Nothing. He led out again, and the troop started down the rocky slope. If he saw nothing by evening, tomorrow they would turn around and head home.

A war cry interrupted his thoughts. Seeing the war tribe hurtling toward them from the right, he shouted for his men to dismount and take cover behind the boulders. The exchange only lasted a few minutes, but by the time the Apache withdrew, he had lost two men and two more were wounded.

The next two days the Apache eluded them, and Jasper had no choice but to assume they had gone to ground. He turned the troop toward home. Eager to see Bessie, he kept a brisk pace back to the fort.

Facing the Apache braves had been an illuminating experience. He wanted children, part of his own flesh and blood to leave behind him. If he had died in the skirmish, would anyone have cared? He thought of Bessie, of his strange marriage. Enough was enough. It was time he was a husband to her.

He didn't think Bessie would object if he asked to move his cot beside hers in the bedroom. But did she love him? He wasn't sure how he felt about her. He admired her and felt a strong liking for her, but was that love?

He was trying to show her biblical love, but it was hard. That was all action, mutual submission, and consideration. Would he ever feel the emotion of strong love, the feeling of being caught up in something bigger than himself? Would he be willing to die for Bessie? The Bible talked about a man loving his wife as Christ loved the church, of offering himself for her. That was a daunting thought.

If they ever hoped to achieve that ideal, they had to make a beginning for a real marriage. He hoped Bessie agreed. The thought of their children around the dinner table or running to greet him when he came home was heartwarming. He wanted lots of children around—little boys with red hair like his own and little girls with Bessie's gray eyes.

The fort seemed unusually quiet when the troops rode in. Several soldiers waved laconically, but most stayed in the few patches of shade. The temperatures were already hovering near one hundred degrees Fahrenheit, and it was only May. What would midsummer be like?

"I'm home," he called, then shut the door behind him. The dim, cooler interior was a welcome relief from the bright heat outside.

The bedroom door opened, and his smile faded when Rooster came out instead of Bessie. "What's wrong? Where's my wife?"

"Settle down, Lieutenant. A rattler took a liking to your missus, and she's been mighty sick. She's yonder in the bed."

A rattler! His heart sank. She was such a tiny thing. Rattlesnake bites could be deadly to children and small or weak adults. He hurried to the bedroom.

Her head propped on pillows, Bessie lay in the bed, her face turned toward the window. She looked so small even though the cot wasn't large. Her translucent skin was so white and fine he thought he could almost see through it. Perspiration beaded on her forehead, and her breathing was erratic. He had seen men bitten before in Texas—she wasn't out of danger yet.

Still asleep, she turned her head, and he sat beside the bed. When he took her hand, it was hot and dry. So small and delicate. He turned it over. Calluses. She never had calluses in Boston, had she? He studied her face. She didn't have that dusting of freckles back at Fort Bridger. She had been a good wife, and she was trying so hard to make a life and a home for him.

He bent his head and prayed for God to spare her. Ruth needed her, and so did he. If this wasn't love, it was as close as he had ever felt. Maybe he wasn't capable of more after being yanked from his family after his mother's death. The way he had been shifted from pillar to post as a child could have stunted his capacity for love, but he felt more for this small woman on the bed than for any other woman who had ever come into his life. For the first time he thanked God he had sent Bessie instead of Lenore.

Jasper stayed beside the bed through the long night. Just before dawn she thrashed in the bedclothes and called his name. "Jasper, don't leave me."

"I'm here, Bessie."

With great effort she opened her eyes and managed to focus on his face. "Don't leave me, Jasper," she whispered. "Please don't send me back to Boston."

He smoothed the hair back from her face. "I wouldn't do that. You're my wife, and we belong together."

"Lenore couldn't love you, you know." Her eyes were bright with fever.

"I know. I'm not interested in Lenore. You are a much better wife."

She seemed to relax at his words, and with an indistinguishable murmur, she fell back asleep. Was that what had been bothering her? Did she think he cared anything about Lenore? From what he had heard of her, he couldn't see Lenore sticking it out in a place like this.

He gazed into Bessie's face. In spite of his intentions to make their marriage a real one, the circumstances prohibited that. Maybe when she was better, they would talk about it.

Bessie winced and shaded her eyes from the sun. She let her gaze travel around the room and come to rest on Jasper. His red head lay inches from her arm. His breathing was deep and regular, and her right hand lay in his. When had he arrived?

For the first time in days she felt clearheaded, though she was still weak and dizzy. She was just glad Ruth was all right. At the thought of her daughter, she glanced around the room again. Where was the baby?

For a moment she panicked. Then she remembered Rooster's presence earlier. He had surely taken the baby. She put her hand on Jasper's hair and twined her fingers in its thick, coarse texture, smiling at her audacity.

He muttered and his eyes opened. The sparkling depth of his gaze made her mouth even drier. She yanked her hand away, and he sat up.

He touched her forehead and smiled. "You're better."

Her heart fluttered at the relief in his voice. "I think so, yes. Where is Ruthie?"

"Rooster has her."

She nodded, but then another thought struck her. "Was she bitten?" Agitated, she raised up on the pillows.

He eased her back. "She's fine. Happy as the soldiers who are spoiling her. I checked on her last night. She was cooing and gurgling with her fist in Rooster's hair."

She relaxed and smiled at the picture.

"The soldiers even got your garden planted." He smoothed her hair. "All you have to do is worry about getting well."

"I'm well." She sat up and ran a hand through her tangled hair. "I must look a sight."

"You're a sight for sore eyes. I missed you and Ruthie while I was gone. We're a family now."

Did he really feel that way? She searched his earnest gaze and saw no deceit. Was this a new beginning for them? She pushed away the specter of her beautiful sister.

Nine

Jasper insisted Bessie rest for a few days. She was relieved at his insistence for she still felt dizzy and light-headed. He brought her the watercolors she had brought with her, and she and Ruth spent daytime hours under the trees along the acequia. She painted scenes of fort life and thought they were pretty good. She captured Rooster and several of the other soldiers that performed drills on the parade ground, the small post band playing their instruments in the cool of the day under the trees near her, and the Indians moving to and from the sutler's store.

For the first time since she had come West, she had time to stop and savor the sights and smells of the fort: the licorice smell of the tobacco plugs the men chewed, the mix and match uniforms they wore, and the fragrance of creosote bushes and sagebrush. She tried to get all that flavor of life down on canvas and was amazed at her own paintings. Her uncle in Boston had urged her to send him some of her work. Perhaps she would send him some of these.

Jasper sometimes joined her with a block of wood and his

whittling knife. They seemed to have made an uneasy truce, uneasy on her end, anyway. He seemed relaxed and content.

$\backsim$

"What are you doing up? I can get my own breakfast," Jasper said.

Bessie jumped. Sometimes he was so noiseless, like a cat. "It's time things got back to normal. I've spent too much time relaxing as it is. It's been two weeks since I've done much of anything. The laundry is piled up, this house is filthy with dust and sand, and we're out of bread."

He grinned. "You could always make more biscuits."

"They might even be edible this time, now that I know how to make them."

He put a hand on her shoulder. "You're doing a fine job. You might make a fair-to-middlin' cook yet." His blue eyes twinkled. "I'm in the mood for beans and corn bread."

She smiled. "That's exactly what I was planning for supper. Where are you going today?"

"We're building new latrines. The commander wants the heavy digging and hard work done before it gets any hotter. Which reminds me. I've arranged for some help for you."

She frowned. "I don't need any help. I'm managing just fine." Did he feel she was failing in some way? She was trying so hard, but her cooking still wasn't great. Jasper ate it without complaint, but maybe he longed for better cooking than she could muster.

"Yes, but I don't want to turn you into a drudge. I want my wife fresh and lively when I come home at night. You have plenty to do just caring for Ruthie. You'll like Eve."

"Who?" she called after him as he walked toward the door.

"Eve. She'll be here soon."

"Another woman?" She couldn't believe it. She had seen no other women since they went through Tucson on the way to Fort Bowie. She felt a sense of excitement tinged with jealousy. Where had he seen this woman, and what had been his true motive in asking for her help?

A soft knock interrupted his answer, and Jasper moved quickly to answer the door. When he opened the door, all Bessie could see over his shoulder was a shining cap of black hair. She smoothed her own brown locks down and hurried forward.

A lovely Indian woman stood on the stoop. Her soft brown eyes were full of trepidation, and her gaze darted from Jasper to Bessie and back again.

"Missus." She bobbed her head and cast her gaze to the ground. "I come to help you with your work." Her English was nearly flawless as was the smooth brown perfection of her skin.

Bessie immediately felt dowdy and unattractive. How could Jasper fail to see how lovely this girl was? Something about her reminded Bessie of Lenore. Perhaps it was the raven hair or the smile. In her mind's eye Bessie could see Jasper and Eve with Ruth. The perfect little family. He had to have hired her because of her beauty.

Stop it! She was behaving like a half-wit.

Jasper frowned and glanced her way, and she realized she was behaving poorly. "Welcome, Eve. Please come in. My husband was just telling me of you." She stepped back from the doorway and motioned her in.

Eve gave Jasper another glance, and she walked past him.

"I'm going now." He brushed Bessie's cheek with his lips and closed the door behind him.

Her cheek burned from the touch of his lips. He did not usually kiss her good-bye in the morning. Was this an attempt to throw her off the rabbit trail her thoughts had taken? Could there be anything between Jasper and this young woman?

Bessie forced a smile. "What do you know how to do, Eve?"

"I can do laundry, clean, cook—anything you need, missus."

"Where did you learn to speak English so well?"

"My mother was white. She met my father, a Navajo chief, when her parents came through on their way to California. My father stole her away, and they were very happy for many years."

"I see." Bessie couldn't imagine such a life for herself. But the woman had evidently never forgotten her roots. She had made sure her daughter spoke English.

"She and your father are still living?"

A shadow crossed Eve's face. "My father died last year. Mother still grieves."

"Where does she live?"

"With my brother and his wife on the reservation."

"I would have thought perhaps she would try to find her white family in California."

Eve shook her head. "She would not be accepted after marrying a Navajo." She said the words matter-of-factly, without a trace of self-pity. "She tried once to write them, but the letter came back. Her parents had rejected it. She threw it away and never spoke of them again."

How terrible it would be never to hear from her parents and family again, to give up a way of life for another and never be able to go back again. "Perhaps you should try to contact them, Eve."

Eve gave her a slight smile. "I think I should begin my work, missus."

In other words, mind your own business. Bessie felt the sting of rebuke. She had been meddling. Her cheeks hot, she led the way to the kitchen.

She showed Eve the washtub and scrub board, but before she could instruct her further, Ruth began to cry. Bessie left Eve in the kitchen and hurried to the baby. "Why is Mama's girl so sad?" she cooed, picking up the infant.

Ruth stopped crying and smiled, reaching out a chubby hand to grasp a tendril of hair.

Bessie smiled tenderly down at the little one. She wanted so much for Ruth, but after talking with Eve, she was fearful. Would people accept her adopted daughter? She snuggled her close and frowned. She could fight some of Ruth's battles, but the child faced a great many more.

Kissing the top of the baby's downy head, she carried her into the kitchen and prepared a bottle for her.

Eve stopped what she was doing and stared at the baby. "She is not white."

"No. I found her with her dead mother in the desert. She is mine now. I love her."

Eve nodded. "It will not be easy, missus."

"Call me Bessie. I would like to be friends." She was surprised to find she no longer felt jealous toward Eve. Jasper would never betray her with this girl. What had she been thinking? Her husband was a man of integrity. Being out in the desert with a man who wanted her sister was making her think unreasonably.

Eve's brows rose. "I am your servant, missus," she said with downcast eyes.

"I need a friend more." Bessie touched Eve's shoulder.

Eve bit her lip. She raised her eyes and met Bessie's gaze. "I, too, need a friend."

"Then let us do our work together, and we can talk as we work. It will make the day go faster."

The day flew by. Eve left before Jasper returned for the evening. She lived with her brother about a mile out of Fort Bowie, and she needed to prepare his supper. When Bessie shut the door behind her new friend, she felt as though she had turned some kind of corner in her acceptance of her new life. Just having a friend made all the difference.

After supper Jasper took out his Bible and studied it while

Bessie did the dishes. She stopped and stared at him through the open doorway. Would she ever get to really know her husband? She loved him now, knew it in every fiber of her being. She loved everything about him. The way his hair grew in a cowlick, the way he played so gently with Ruthie, the sweet, kind things he did for her. Just like hiring Eve. He had only been thinking of her, but Bessie's first thought had been of suspicion. He was solicitous of her health and well-being, but what did he really feel?

Bessie thought again of the letter hidden in the bottom of his mess chest. She desired to know its contents but feared to read it. So far she had resisted the temptation and hoped she was strong enough to continue.

After drying her hands on her apron, she took it off and hung it on a peg on the wall. She smoothed her hair and joined Jasper in the parlor.

He smiled when she sat beside him. "Ruthie sleeping already?"

"Like a lamb. She won't wake until morning."

He stretched out his legs and sighed. "I'm bushed."

"Hard day?"

He nodded. "That sun saps me. But the latrines are dug. How did it go with Eve today?"

Bessie could feel her spirits lift at the mere mention of her friend. "Wonderfully! Did you know her mother is white?"

Jasper looked surprised. "I had no idea. Did she tell you that?"

Bessie leaned back. "She doesn't have to live on the reservation because she is part white. Her mother still lives there, even though Eve's father is dead."

"Understandable. She would be ostracized back East."

"Even out here?"

"They might be polite to her face, but they would likely talk about her behind her back. Men would think she was fair game, and women would think she was no better than a common street girl. She's better to stay where she is."

Bessie frowned. "What about Ruthie?"

Jasper sighed. "It won't be easy, Bessie. I hope and pray things change by the time Ruthie grows up." He put an arm around her and hugged her. "Let's not borrow trouble yet. We'll do the best we can, pray, and leave it in God's hands."

She leaned against him and marveled at how safe she felt in his arms. He pulled her closer and propped his chin on her head. She could hear his heart beating under her ear and smell the scent of horse and leather on his uniform.

"Hey, I almost forgot to tell you. The stage brought news about the impeachment. President Johnson was acquitted because the Senate didn't have a two-thirds majority. The vote was thirty-five for impeachment and nineteen for acquittal."

She didn't care about politics. It seemed very far away, especially tonight. Back in Boston her father would be arguing with his cronies over the vote, and papers would be full of screaming headlines. Her world had shrunk to this man and the baby in the other room. It seemed a fair trade to Bessie.

"Are you ready for our study tonight?"

His grip around her shoulders relaxed, and she pulled away with reluctance. "What are we looking at tonight?" They were still going through 1 Corinthians 13 and cross-referencing it with other verses.

"Verse 7 says, 'Beareth all things, believeth all things, hopeth all things, endureth all things.' I found a reference there to Galatians 6, verse 2. 'Bear ye one another's burdens, and so fulfil the law of Christ.'" He cupped her cheek. "Can you share any of your burdens with me, Bessie? I'll try my best to help you carry them. You've seemed distant for a while. Is it something I've done or failed to do?"

She longed to tell him she had found that letter, but she couldn't. She just couldn't bear to bring Lenore into this house by talking about her. Jasper never mentioned her, but did he find his wife a poor substitute for the woman he really wanted? She suspected he did, but she didn't want her fears confirmed.

She smiled into his blues eyes. "It's been an adjustment." Which was true. It had been hard to make the transition from Boston to here. She hoped he would accept that.

His expression softened, and he nodded. "You've been gently reared, and dealing with scorpions, snakes, and spiders has not been fun. Have you written your family lately? I know you haven't received any letters. Would you like to go visit them for the summer?"

Was he trying to get rid of her? She swallowed past the lump in her throat. "No. My place is with you. Mother promised they would try to visit next year. I'll be fine. I want to be here."

Relief filled his face. Her heart sped up at the realization that he didn't want her to go.

"What do you want out of our marriage and our life together, Bessie?"

Did she dare tell him? Did she dare say she wanted his love and his children, the joy of teaching their children about Jesus and growing old together? He would think her forward if she mentioned children now. But where was her courage? She had always been timid and unsure, but out here she was more courageous than she had ever been.

She took a deep breath. "I want—" She broke off at the wail from the bedroom.

"Uh-oh, I thought you said she was out for the night."

"Ruthie had to prove me wrong, didn't she?" Bessie stood and walked toward the bedroom. "I won't be long. I'm sure she'll go right back to sleep."

Bessie laid a soothing hand on Ruth and sang to her gently. The baby corked her thumb in her mouth and went right back to sleep. What had disturbed her? Was it a sign from God that she shouldn't tell Jasper how she felt yet?

Tears burned her eyes. She didn't know how much longer she could go on the way things were. Even if Jasper never loved her, if she could just muster the courage to speak, Bessie could have the comfort of raising their children.

She straightened her shoulders and made her way back to the parlor. Jasper looked up from his perusal of his Bible and smiled. "Everything all right?"

"Fine. I don't know what woke her."

He patted the space beside him. "Come finish our conversation."

His gaze followed her every movement, and she felt self-conscious as she walked to the cot and sat next to him. He immediately put his arm around her, and she forced her shoulders to relax. Together they leaned against the wall.

"Do you have anything to say about my question?" he asked, his words muffled by his lips in her hair.

Her heart pounded. It was now or never. An opportunity might not come this way again. "I want to have a family, children that we raise for God." A whisper was all her dry throat could manage. "What do you want from our marriage?"

Jasper stilled. His heart beat beneath her ear, and now it sped up. She heard him catch his breath, then he tilted her face and gazed into her eyes. "Children? You want children too?"

Did he mean he wanted children? Her eyes searched his. Did she dare ask him how he really felt about her? He was doing all the right things, but was it out of a sense of duty or out of genuine emotion? She opened her mouth to ask, but the impetuous words were stilled by a knock on the door.

"Lieutenant Mendenhall!" Someone pounded on their door.

Jasper gave her a rueful glance and got up to answer the door. He came back moments later. "I have to go. There's been an attack

on some settlers south of here. I'll probably be gone a few days."
He knelt and took her face in his hands. "We'll talk of this when I
return." He kissed her briefly and took his hat.

Bessie willed him to look back and smile just one last time, but
without looking at her, he shut the door behind him.

Ten

The stars twinkled in the night like pinpoints of hope against the dark velvet sky. Jasper led the detachment along the rocky trail and thought about what had just happened with Bessie. He was glad of the interruption. Her admission that she wanted children had rocked him. It was what he wanted, too, but to hear her admit it seemed like a gift from God.

They came over a rise. Orange flames still smoldered in the burned and blackened cabin below them. Grimly, Jasper led the way to the cabin. He didn't want to see what condition the settlers would be in. They were probably dead.

They were almost to the cabin when he heard a wail off to his right. He wheeled his mare and spurred her toward the sound. Beside a small stream gleaming in the moonlight, a woman crouched over the body of a man and a child. Keening in grief, she rocked back and forth on her heels.

He touched her shoulder, and she whipped around with a long-bladed knife in her hand.

"You're safe, ma'am!" He sprang back, then grappled with her and finally succeeded in wresting the knife from her grasp. She fell atop the two bodies and resumed her wailing.

He pulled her away, and she didn't resist this time. Leading her away from the carnage, he motioned to Rooster to bring him the spare horse they had brought with them. Her head rolled back as he lifted her onto the horse, and he saw with shock that she could have been Lenore's twin. He almost snatched his fingers away, then assisted her to the ground. This poor lady had just lost her entire family, and he was letting a simple resemblance get in the way of his compassion.

He would take her to Bessie before pursuing the savages who did this. His wife's gentle touch would help this lady. He told Rooster to load the bodies and bring them back to the fort for burial. He then helped the woman into the saddle. She slumped against the gelding's neck, and he swung into his own saddle and started back to Fort Bowie.

Their quarters were dark when he helped the woman inside. He shut the door and fumbled as he lit the lantern. "Bessie," he called.

The woman started when he spoke, and he laid a soothing hand on her arm. "It's all right. My wife will be here in a moment."

Moments later Bessie came running from the bedroom, her hair falling to her waist and her eyes frightened. "Jasper? What's wrong?"

Her gaze went to his hand on the woman's arm, and he

withdrew it hastily. "This woman has lost her family to Cochise and his band. Can you care for her? I have to go after them."

Bessie stepped closer, and her face blanched. "Lenore?" she asked in a trembling voice.

"No, not Lenore, but I saw the resemblance too." He stepped away and Bessie stepped closer. "I must go." He stared at his wife uneasily as the color began to come back into her cheeks.

"You poor dear." She went to the woman and put her arm around her shoulders. "Come with me. I'll fix you some tea."

The woman allowed Bessie to lead her to the kitchen, and Jasper sighed in relief. He would have the men give the bodies a decent burial, and Bessie would take care of the woman.

Bessie's hands trembled as she poured the boiling water into the teapot. The woman's resemblance to her sister was uncanny! Why would God bring such a reminder into her home when Lenore's memory was finally dulling in Jasper's mind?

What an uncharitable thought. This poor woman had no control over her appearance. How could Bessie be thinking such things when this woman had just lost everything? She was ashamed of herself.

She set the cup in front of the woman. The poor lady stared into space vacantly, then tears began to flow, leaving clean rivulets in her smoke-blackened face.

Bessie touched her hand. "Have some tea. You don't have to talk about what happened."

The woman sobbed softly. "Oh, it was terrible! My poor little Danny! And James." Her sobs grew louder, and she rocked back and forth in her grief.

She could feel this woman's pain. If something happened to Ruthie or Jasper, how could she bear it? What could she say now to comfort this woman?

After nearly an hour of racking sobs, the woman brought herself under control. She took several deep breaths and raised reddened eyes to meet Bessie's gaze. "You're very kind. Was that your husband who brought me here? I don't remember much." She closed her eyes with the strain of trying to control her emotions.

"Yes, that was my husband. I'm Bessie Mendenhall, and my husband is Jasper."

"I'm Myra Trimble." She dabbed at her eyes again. "James always said my name didn't fit me. It means tearful, and he had never seen me cry. Now, he never will." She bowed her head in a fresh spasm of weeping.

Bessie knelt and put her arms around Myra. "I know it hurts," she murmured. "Let it out." She patted her back and cried with her. The mere thought of losing Jasper and Ruthie brought a hard knot to her stomach.

Myra finally pulled away and fished in her sleeve for her handkerchief. "I've always been so stoic and strong. Now I can't seem to stop crying." She took a deep breath. "The vision of my son lying beside his father burns in my brain. I can't get it out."

"God has your husband and son in the palm of his hand. You can rest in that."

Myra's lips tightened. "Don't talk to me of a God who would allow my two-year-old son to be slaughtered! I want nothing to do with a God like that." Hectic spots of color stained her cheeks, and she took her cold tea and swallowed it in a gulp.

The poor woman didn't even have faith to help her through this. Pity for Myra overwhelmed Bessie. How did one deal with a tragedy of this magnitude without faith? But she wouldn't argue with her. Maybe her short stay with them would open her eyes to eternal things. Bessie prayed for wisdom to say the right things in the next few days.

After she got Myra situated on the couch cot, Bessie went to bed. She tossed and turned for a long time before sleep claimed her exhausted body.

When Ruth whimpered and cried out, Bessie groaned and opened her eyes to the dawn light. She wasn't ready for morning. It had to have been after two o'clock before she got to bed. She reached over and put her hand in the cradle. Ruth grabbed her finger and brought it to her mouth. She sucked on it greedily, and Bessie laughed.

"All right, you slave driver, I'm getting your breakfast." Eve would be here soon too. The thought of her friend lightened her heart. She had two women today. Though she wouldn't call Myra a friend yet. The woman's bitterness against God separated her from Bessie. But Bessie determined to be the best friend she could to the bereaved woman.

She climbed out of bed and quickly dressed in her lightest dress. July was almost here, and the day already promised to be a scorcher. She picked up Ruth and went to the kitchen. By the time she had fed her and put her on the floor on a blanket, Eve was knocking gently on the back door.

"We have a guest," Bessie warned her quietly when she let her in. "A widow from an attack last night."

A shadow crossed Eve's face. "Perhaps I should go. She will not wish to see me today after such a thing."

"She can't possibly blame you. You had nothing to do with an attack by Apache braves."

Eve shrugged. "I see it many times, my friend. To some whites, the only good Indian is a dead one."

Bessie had heard that expression many times, but it still pained her. "Don't go. I was so looking forward to seeing you."

Eve smiled. "I too. Very well, if you wish it, I will stay. But do not say I did not warn you."

They soon had the kitchen and bedroom cleaned as they waited for Myra to awaken. It was nearly ten o'clock before they heard her stirring. Bessie went to the parlor to greet her.

"Good morning," she said with a smile. "We have tea and bis-cuits for breakfast. Are you hungry?"

Myra sat up and pushed her hair back from her face. In

the daylight she didn't look quite so much like Lenore, but the resemblance was still there. The same raven hair, sultry eyes, and pouting mouth.

"That sounds lovely." Her expression wooden and grave, she slipped out of bed and followed Bessie to the kitchen. She stopped short when she saw Eve and little Ruth. Venom and rage chased one another over her face. "Indians!" she spat out. Her hands curved like claws, and she started toward Eve.

Bessie sprang after her and only succeeded in stopping her with great difficulty. "Eve is my friend. She had nothing to do with your loss."

"All savages are the same," Myra said, glaring at Eve. "If she didn't do this one, she likely had a hand in others."

"No, you must calm down, Myra. Have some tea." Bessie forced her into a chair and hurried to get the tea and biscuits.

Myra pointed a shaking finger at Eve. "You wouldn't be telling me to calm down if that were your husband and child she and those murderers had butchered." She glared at Eve again, then slumped back in her chair.

Bessie sighed when the agitation seeped out of Myra's manner. She set the tea and biscuits on the table in front of her guest. "Is there someone we can telegraph for you? Family somewhere?"

Myra didn't look at Eve again. She picked up a biscuit. "I should let my brother know. He has a ranch near Tucson. And our parents, I suppose. They live in Boston."

"I'm from Boston!"

Myra looked her fully in the face for the first time. "You are? We lived in Boston until a year ago when James decided to come out here. I tried to warn him, but he wouldn't listen." She sighed and stared into her teacup.

The similarities choked Bessie for a moment. Did tragedy await her somewhere down the road? She hadn't wanted to come here either. For a moment she felt as though a heavy weight lay on her chest. She wanted to run out of the house, find the nearest stage, and head for home. She took a deep breath and sat cautiously beside Myra.

She must not let Myra realize how much her words had shaken her. They chatted about Boston for a few minutes, but she could sense the rage simmering in Myra just below the surface. Bessie pitied her, but she did not really like her. Her anger unsettled Bessie.

Ruth let out a mewling gurgle, and Myra's head swiveled toward the sound. Her eyes narrowed, and she looked at Eve. "Your brat?"

Bessie's throat tightened. Their brief truce was obviously over. "She's mine. She's a darling. I found her with her dead mother in the desert and adopted her."

"You should have left her to die," Myra spat out. "To lie out under the blazing sun just like my Danny." She began to weep again and left the room with a venomous look over her shoulder.

Shaken, Bessie looked at Eve. "What should we do?" she whispered. She didn't want Myra to hear her and launch into another tirade.

Eve shrugged. "She will have to deal with this in her own

way," she said softly. "Do not fret over my feelings. I am used to it." She turned and got out the ingredients for the stew they had decided to prepare for supper.

The next morning Bessie and Myra filed to the burial of Myra's husband and son. She left Ruthie in Eve's care. Myra's eyes glared balefully from a face devoid of color. She didn't cry, not even when the small wooden coffin containing the remains of her son was lowered into the scarred earth. Bessie wept for her, though. She could only imagine how much pain cried to be released from the other woman's heart.

The next few days were like living in an armed camp. Bessie had to watch everything Myra did. She didn't trust her around Eve or Ruth. Ruth cried every time she came near, as if she sensed her animosity.

Bessie longed for Jasper to return. She needed his strength and wisdom to handle this situation. Meanwhile Myra made no mention of leaving. Why couldn't she go to her brother in Tucson? What held her here? For just a moment Bessie wondered if Myra wanted to see Jasper again, but she pushed the thought away. What was she thinking? The woman had just lost her husband and small son.

After waiting in expectation for nearly a week, Bessie heard the commotion of the returning detachment. She hurried to the door. "Jasper is back."

"Newlyweds, are you?" Myra said with a sly smile. "Don't worry, honey, that excitement will wear off soon enough. You'll soon be looking forward to times away from him."

Bessie didn't bother answering. She would always long to be with Jasper. When she heard the back door close, she was glad Myra had the sense to leave so she could greet Jasper alone.

The baby didn't give a peep either in the half hour Bessie waited for Jasper. Finally she heard his step on the front stoop and hurried to open the door.

He looked dusty and tired, but he smiled when he saw her. He held out his arms, and she rushed into them. "I missed my girls."

"We missed you. Did you find Cochise?"

He shook his head. "Not a trace. He hides in those Dragoon Mountains like a snake." He removed his hat and followed her inside. "How did you get along with the widow? I don't even know her name."

"It's Myra Trimble. She's still very distressed." She wanted to blurt out her fear of the woman, but what if he thought she was being foolish? It would be better if he saw for himself.

"Is she still here?" Jasper looked past her into the kitchen.

"Yes. She has a brother in Tucson, but she hasn't seemed in any hurry to go to her family. I'm not sure why. She hates Eve."

He frowned. "Because she's Navajo? Not surprising under the circumstances, I guess. What about Ruthie? Is she all right with her?"

"I'm not comfortable with the way she looks at the baby. She's so strange, Jasper. Full of bitterness and anger. She hates God."

He hugged her. "Sounds like you've been under siege."

"It's felt like it at times."

"Where's my girl? Sleeping?"

Bessie nodded. "I'll get her."

"No, don't wake her up. I just was wondering if she'll recognize me. She'll be cranky if you wake her."

She laughed. "That baby doesn't have a cranky bone in her body. She's outgrown that cradle too. Her feet were sticking out the ends, and her poor little head bumped the headboard. I've had her sleeping with me. I pushed the cot up against the wall so she won't fall out."

"I'll find her another bed by tomorrow."

His gaze brought the heat to her cheeks. Did he mean to begin their marriage in earnest tomorrow? Her mouth went dry. Surely not. Myra would be in the next room. It would be too embarrassing. But soon, his expression promised. She smiled uncertainly.

"I think I'll check on Ruthie." She could sense his gaze on her as she hurried from the room. Why did she always run when things got too intense? She was a coward. She should have stayed, melted in his arms, and kissed him.

She opened the door to the bedroom and stared at the bed blankly. Was Ruth covered by the blanket? She couldn't see even her little rump sticking up through the bedclothes. Bessie went to the bed and felt it. Empty. She whirled and looked around. Had Ruthie fallen out? Bessie looked under the bed and over every inch of floor space before she began to panic.

"Jasper!"

He came immediately. "What is it? What's wrong?"

"I can't find Ruthie," she gasped. "She isn't anywhere in the bedroom."

"She has to be. Let's look again. Was she in the bed?"

Bessie nodded. Perhaps she was mistaken, and she had put Ruthie down for her nap on the cot in the parlor. But the tiny parlor was as empty as the bedroom. No Ruthie.

"She has to be here. No one would take her." Jasper joined her in the parlor.

At his words the blood drained from Bessie's face, and she felt faint. "Myra!"

Eleven

Jasper tried to tell himself that no woman would harm a child, even her worst enemy's. But Bessie's terror soon communicated itself to him. He sent for Eve. She could help keep Bessie calm while he mounted a search.

"It's my fault, my fault," Bessie wailed. "I knew she was unbalanced. I didn't like the way she looked at Ruthie. I should have known to keep the baby with me at all times."

"It's not your fault," he told her. "You couldn't have known she would take the baby with you right there in the house."

"Lieutenant."

They both looked up at the sound. Rooster stood in the doorway, his face filled with concern. "I've found tracks, sir. They're heading toward the Dragoon Mountains."

"On foot?" Would Myra be so crazy?

"No, sir. She's mounted. She stole a horse from the corral while Private Montel took a siesta."

Which just proved her craziness. What person in her right mind would head off into the desert during the worst heat of the day in one of the hottest months of the year? Jasper's fear for his adopted daughter increased. What did the woman plan to do? And why head right into Cochise's territory? It *was* madness.

Eve rushed in the door, and Bessie threw herself into her arms. "She's taken my baby," she sobbed.

Eve patted her back and soothed her. "I was with my brother when Jasper sent for me. My brother has gathered some braves, and they are searching too. He will find her." Eve's gaze met Jasper's, and he saw fear. The desert was a big place, and Ruth was just a tiny baby at the mercy of a madwoman. What if Myra got it into her head to leave the baby somewhere to die in the heat? The thought tormented him.

He thought of their laughter the day she learned to roll over, the little birthmark shaped like a butterfly on the inside of one chubby knee, and the way her brown eyes widened when she saw him, followed by her slow smile and reaching hands. He had to find their baby.

Bessie followed Jasper to the door. She thrust a full pillowcase in his hands. "Here, take this. There are diapers, clean clothes, and her bottle. It's full."

She buried her face in his shirt, and he hugged her fiercely. "Pray, Bessie. Pray for all you're worth." He kissed the top of her head and left her with Eve.

The scorching sun beat down, and he flinched at the heat. How could a frail woman withstand hours of this with no shade? She did not even have a hat. And Ruthie's tender skin would be exposed to the sun. He found his mare already saddled and led the detachment toward the Dragoon Mountains. Rooster could follow a hawk's shadow where it fell on the sand, or at least that's how Jasper felt sometimes. The old man was the best tracker Jasper knew.

They had followed the trail for fifteen minutes when Rooster pointed. "Sandstorm coming."

"We have to find them before it hits!" The storm would wipe away any trace of prints. It would likely kill Myra and the baby too. She didn't have enough sense to seek shelter, what little shelter there was.

Rooster pointed again. "We can shelter there, behind the horses."

Rooster was right. Jasper was responsible for the safety of his men, but his heart was almost unbearably heavy as he turned his mare's face and led the men to the rock face Rooster had pointed out. All hope was lost. What could he tell Bessie?

They positioned the horses in front of them and knelt and covered their faces with their coats. The wind was upon them in moments, driving the sand into any exposed skin like tiny biting insects. Jasper prayed as he knelt there. All he could see was Bessie's face when she realized the baby was gone. She would blame herself if he didn't find Ruth. He didn't think she could live with that.

The storm was over nearly as quickly as it started. The sun

came out and the wind died down. Jasper stood and ordered the men to saddle up and get ready to ride.

"Where to, Lieutenant?"

Rooster's gaze met his, and he nearly flinched at the resignation he saw there. They might never even find the small corpse. "All we can do is go in the direction we last saw her tracks."

Rooster sighed. "Even the biggest ball of twine unravels. But with the good Lord's help, maybe we can rewind this one."

Jasper looked at him askance. "This was a small storm. With a bit of luck we may pick up their trail on the other side."

Jasper didn't think Rooster thought it a likely occurrence, but it was better than no hope at all.

They plodded through the rocky sand but found no trace of a trail. At dusk Jasper had no choice but to call off the search for the night. The thought of little Ruth spending the night in the desert was almost more than he could bear. Dangerous creatures came out at night. Rattlesnakes and scorpions. He prayed for her safety as he unrolled his bedroll and lay out under the stars.

Starting at every sound, Bessie paced the floor restlessly. How could Ruth still be alive? But the tiny flame of hope refused to die. Jasper would find her. He loved her too. So did the men. Rooster could track anything, and they had some of their best men with them. If anyone could bring back her baby, that detachment could.

Eve refused to leave her, although Bessie urged her to go home. Several of the soldiers stopped by to see if they could do anything for her. Even Major Daniels sent over a note urging her to call on him if she needed anything. She knew many of them thought she should not have kept Ruth, but in this hour of need, they rallied around her.

Four days and nights had dragged by. Bessie couldn't eat, couldn't sleep. If she just knew what was happening. If only Jasper had allowed her to go! She understood, of course, that it simply was too dangerous. But that fact did not make the wait any easier. Eve talked her into going to bed, but all she did was doze off and on.

❧

The morning after the sandstorm, Jasper awoke gritty eyed and discouraged. He dumped the spoiled milk for the baby, and they quickly broke camp and mounted up. As dusk fell for the second night, he knew they would have to start back if they did not find signs of Myra tomorrow. They were almost to the Dragoon Mountains, and he didn't have enough men to hold off Cochise's warriors.

As they were saddling up the next morning, the scout gave a shout. "Indians, Lieutenant!"

Jasper vaulted into his saddle and grabbed his rifle. As he wheeled to face the charge, he realized they weren't hostile Indians. The Indians plodded toward them without weapons drawn. He shielded his eyes and tried to see what they were up to.

As they came nearer, one held up a hand. "Lieutenant Mendenhall!"

They knew his name? This one spoke perfect English. Jasper squinted in the bright morning sun. The man looked vaguely familiar. He reminded Jasper of Eve. This must be her brother. As they came closer he saw the man was holding something. A glimpse of dark hair brought his heart to his throat. Was that Ruthie?

He urged his horse toward the band and stopped in front of the leader. The man was smiling, and Jasper could see the resemblance to Eve even more clearly.

The Indian reined in his horse and held out the baby. "Is this small one what you searched for?"

Jasper took her and snuggled her close. She opened her eyes and smiled her slow smile and gurgled. Tears pricked his eyes. "How can I thank you?"

The man smiled. "I am Ben, brother to Eve. You have been kind to my sister. We always pay our debts."

"What about the woman Myra?"

A mask of stone came down over Ben's face. "She is no more. Cochise and his warriors found her before I did. She resides beneath the earth with her husband and son now."

Jasper searched for the capacity to feel pity for the woman and was surprised to find himself capable of it. She had been driven mad by grief. "How did you get Ruthie?"

"I told Cochise she had been stolen from her mother, and I would return her. She cried, and he was glad to give her to me."

Ben grinned and patted Ruth's silky head. "He did not ask about the mother, and I did not tell him."

Jasper held out his hand. "Thank you, my friend."

Ben shook it. "You will need this for the trip." He handed over a sheepskin of milk and a cup made out of a gourd.

"Can she drink from the cup?" Jasper asked doubtfully.

"She does not like it, but she drinks. It will do until she is in her mother's arms." Ben nodded to the Navajo braves with him, and they all filed away.

Jasper tucked Ruth in his left arm. The sooner they got to the fort, the better.

Bessie woke when the sentry called the midnight hour. She sat up and looked around. Something had awakened her. What was it? Not the sentry. She was used to that. She listened closely, then went to the door. It sounded like horses and voices.

At Bessie's first movement Eve opened her eyes on her pallet on the floor and joined her at the door. Bessie opened it, and they both stepped out onto the front stoop. The moon was so bright it was almost as light as dusk.

"What is it?" Eve whispered.

Bessie squinted through the moonlit night and thought she saw horses milling around in front of the stagecoach station. She was still dressed, even down to her boots, so she started across the parade ground. Eve followed her.

As she neared the group she heard a familiar cry and then Jasper's voice. Her pulse beat wildly in her throat, and a sob burst from her lips. Jasper turned with Ruth in his arms. He grinned from ear to ear.

She leaped forward with arms outstretched. "Ruthie!"

The baby gurgled and reached out chubby fingers for her. "Mummm, mummm," she chortled.

Bessie gathered her into her arms and buried her face in the baby's chubby neck. She smelled like sweat, urine, and sour milk, but Bessie had never smelled a flower or a sachet that smelled more wonderful. She kissed her over and over again while Jasper looked on with an indulgent smile. Ruthie soon tired of the attention and began to fuss.

Bessie turned to Jasper with shining eyes. "I knew you would find her." Her smile encompassed all the tired men. "Thank you all so much. I'll never forget what you've done."

"I wish I could take the credit, but you have to thank someone else." Jasper nodded to Eve. "Eve's brother Ben found her. Cochise's braves had already killed Myra, and they had Ruthie. They'd been taking good care of her: She was clean and well fed. They even sent back some milk for her, but it's all gone now, and I ran out of clean clothes. She's probably hungry. Ben managed to talk Cochise into letting him take the baby."

This was a debt she could never repay. Bessie turned to Eve. "My friend, what can I say?"

Eve smiled. "No words are necessary with friends."

Bessie kissed her on the cheek. "Thank you." She turned back to Jasper. "She needs a bath and bed."

He grimaced. "I know. So do I."

She was stricken with conscience. She hadn't even thought of how tired he must be. The lines of exhaustion around his nose and mouth smote her like a blow. "I'll heat some water."

He gave her another tired smile. "I'll be along in a minute." He turned to thank his men again.

Bessie hurried back home. Home. It truly was home again. Their little family was safe and complete once more.

She saw the Indian who worked with the soldiers making adobe and waved. He had always taken a special interest in Ruth. He would be glad to know the baby was safely home. He nodded gravely. Several soldiers had come out to see what the commotion was, and they clapped when she walked by with the baby.

After Bessie fed Ruthie, she fetched the bathtub down from the wall in the bedroom and poured hot water into it, while Eve hauled more water from the acequia. They filled the washtub for Ruth and the bathtub for Jasper. She stripped Ruth and plunked her into the warm water. The baby gurgled and kicked, and Bessie laughed. Everything seemed normal again.

Although she didn't want to let the baby out of her sight, she handed her to Eve to dress and went to lay out a towel for Jasper. She heard him come in while she was in the bedroom.

She was testing the water when he shut the door behind him. "I'm bushed. All I want is a hot bath and bed."

"Are you hungry?"

He shook his head. "Too tired to be hungry. I wouldn't turn down a cup of coffee, though."

"I'll make some." She turned to go, but he laid his hand on her arm.

"We're a family now, aren't we, Bessie?"

"Yes," she said softly. "We're a family now."

Was a near disaster needed to make them both see the treasure found in these four walls? She felt an overwhelming sense of gratitude to God that they finally had seen it.

She sensed his gaze on her as she let herself out and shut the door behind her. By the time the coffee was ready, Jasper should be done with his bath. Ruthie was already asleep on the cot in the parlor with Eve.

Bessie's cheeks went hot. Eve evidently had assumed Jasper slept in the bed with her and thought it would be okay to go to bed with the baby. What was she to do? Her mouth dry, Bessie poured Jasper a cup of coffee and tapped on the bedroom door.

"Come on in. I'm decent."

She cautiously pushed open the door and found him dressed in long johns, his hair sticking up on end. "Here's your coffee."

He took it with a smile of thanks that faded when he looked at her. "What's wrong?"

Was she that easy to read? She gulped. "Eve and Ruthie are already asleep on the cot in the parlor."

His gaze grew soft, but he didn't say anything for a long moment. "The sun took everything out of me. You're safe. It will be a squeeze, but that cot will hold both of us, if you don't mind." His words were gentle.

Her face burned with humiliation. Did he think she planned it this way? They had never had a chance to finish their discussion of her desire for children. He stared at her, but she couldn't read his expression. "I don't mind," she said softly.

His expression softened further. "I'll be asleep before you even get ready for bed."

She nodded, not daring to meet his gaze. She quickly gathered her things and went to the kitchen. She shivered as she took off her dress, hung it on a hook by the door, and pulled on her nightdress. Then she took her hair down and slipped back inside the bedroom.

Jasper lay along the edge, exhaustion etched in his face. He breathed deeply, already sleeping. Bessie blew out the candle and felt the end of the bed. She crept along the wall to the pillow and then slipped beneath the bedclothes. The desert night was cool, but her shivering wasn't just from the chill. Her husband's warmth spread toward her like a welcoming hug, and she snuggled inside.

It felt strange and wonderful at the same time. She allowed herself to relax. Reaching out a tentative hand, she touched his arm. Knowing he was sleeping, she gathered her courage and slid closer and pillowed her head on his shoulder. The sound of his deep breaths relaxed her further, and it wasn't long before she slipped into the welcome arms of sleep.

Twelve

Jasper yawned. Every bone in his body ached, and his eyes felt swollen from hours of staring into the hot sun. He started to move and discovered his arm was trapped. Startled, he looked down and saw Bessie sleeping with her head on his shoulder. He smiled.

He stared at his sleeping wife. She looked so lovely, so peaceful. And she was his. Why had he ever thought she didn't compare to the picture of Lenore? Her sister's image had dimmed in his mind, and he could barely remember what she looked like. Her hair was darker, wasn't it? He picked up a lock of Bessie's fine light-brown hair and rubbed it between his fingers. It felt like strands of silk. He brought it to his nose and inhaled the fresh scent. Eve had shown her how to make shampoo from yucca, and they had added some flowers.

Her skin was white and fine pored with a hint of pink to her cheeks. And she was so small. Protectiveness filled him as he stroked her face before slipping out of bed. He glanced at Bessie's sleeping face once more while he pulled on his clothes, then reluctantly opened the door and stepped into the kitchen.

Eve was feeding Ruth, and he patted the infant on the head before moving to the stove. He poured a cup of coffee, took it back to the table, and sat across from Eve.

"Bessie is exhausted. Please let her sleep."

"Of course." Eve pulled the bottle from Ruth's slack mouth. The infant sighed but didn't awaken. "She will not sleep long, though. She will wish to see Ruthie soon."

He nodded. Bessie was a good mother. And a good wife. She tried so hard, and he didn't always appreciate her efforts. God had given them a miracle by preserving little Ruth through this ordeal.

The door opened, and Bessie came out from the bedroom rubbing the sleep from her eyes. Her hair was tousled, and she still wore her nightgown. Her gaze skittered away from Jasper, and he realized she was embarrassed. She quickly went to Ruth and knelt beside the chair.

Touching the baby's soft head, she laid her lips on her forehead. "Is she all right?"

"Just sleeping." Eve handed the baby to Bessie and rose. "I would like to return home and thank my brother for finding Ruth. Is that all right?"

Bessie gripped her hand. "I would like to thank him myself. Please convey my heartfelt gratitude."

"And mine." Jasper knew he would have come home bereaved and empty-handed if it hadn't been for Ben. He would not have been able to bear the grief in Bessie's eyes.

Eve smiled and squeezed her hand. "I will be back this afternoon."

"Take the entire day," Bessie urged her. "You haven't slept in days either. None of us will do much today. I'm not going to let Ruthie out of my sight."

Eve nodded. "In the morning, then." She smiled once more and hurried away.

Jasper stared at Bessie until she finally looked up and met his gaze. "Did you sleep well?"

Color tinged her fair skin, and she looked away. "Very well, thank you. You?"

"I didn't move all night." How did he go about bringing up the fact that he wanted their sleeping arrangements to continue? It was so awkward. Perhaps he would wait until tonight. He hated his cowardice.

"What are your plans for the day?"

She smiled and looked down at the baby. "Nothing except spending time with Ruthie."

"I think I'll do the same. My eyes still burn from the sun, and last night the colonel told me to take the day off. Is there any heavy lifting or something special you're needing done that I can help you with?"

"Well, I have been wanting to move the furniture out and clean under it and behind it. Your mess chest is heavy."

"I can do that." He was happy there was something she needed from him. He wished he knew how she really felt. But did it matter? They were married, and they would build a life together. It was as simple as that. He enjoyed the thought of spending the day with his small family.

She put Ruth on the cot, and Jasper made a mental note to get a crib made for her.

"Well, boss, what do we do first?" he asked when she came back.

"Let's move your mess chest underneath the window. Then we can use it as a window seat."

He nodded and went to shove it across the parlor floor. As he put his hand behind it, he felt a sticky substance and jerked his hand away. A shiny black spider raced toward his fingers. Bessie screamed, and he jumped farther away. The spider disappeared behind the chest.

"It was a black widow, wasn't it?" Bessie said fearfully.

He nodded. "I knew as soon as I felt that sticky web. That's why I pulled my hand away so fast."

"We have to kill it. What if it should bite Ruthie?"

"Get me a shoe. I'll get a shovel to pull the chest out with."

She bit her lip and hurried to the bedroom while he went out the back door and grabbed a shovel. He hated spiders. Back in Texas he had seen his share of tarantulas, and they never failed to spook him. Black widows were more dangerous and fast. If he had hesitated at all, this one would have nailed him. But he was glad he had been there. If Bessie had tried to move the chest herself, she would have been bitten.

Bessie wasn't in the parlor when he returned. "Hey, where are you?" he called.

Her muffled voice floated through the bedroom door. "I'm getting dressed. I want all the layers of clothing possible between me and that spider. And I'm trying to decide which shoe to use. I don't want to use one of mine. I would probably never wear it again."

He chuckled. "I'll protect you."

She opened the door. Her hair was still disheveled, but she had her boots on and wore a determined expression. She carried one of his work boots in one hand and the broom in the other.

"You look like you're loaded for bear." He grinned. "Have you had experience in spider hunting before?"

"Many times. And I've killed more scorpions than I can count since we've been here." Her shoulders stiff with purpose, she advanced into the room.

"You've never mentioned it," he said in surprise. But why was he surprised? She had proven herself more than equal to any task so far.

"I knew I had to learn to handle these kinds of things if I expected to be a helpmeet." She shrugged.

An altogether remarkable woman. He smiled and moved to the mess chest again. "Maybe you'd better move Ruthie to the bedroom. If that thing decides to run, there's no telling where it may end up."

Bessie looked alarmed and snatched the baby up. Ruth stirred but didn't awaken as Bessie took her to the bedroom.

Jasper waited until she returned. "Ready? I'm going to use the shovel to pull the chest out. When the spider comes out, smack it with the broom to stun it enough so I can kill it."

Her face was white, but she nodded. "Ready."

If he didn't hate them so much, Jasper would have felt pity for the spider. Bessie held the broom between both hands like a bat, and he suspected she would deliver a mighty whop with it. He thrust the shovel behind the mess chest and pushed it out from the wall with one strong shove. Several black blobs raced up the back of the chest. "Here they come!"

"They?"

Her eyes widened in horror but she stood like a miniature Joan of Arc, her feet planted with the broom instead of a sword, ready to strike. He would have laughed if the situation hadn't been so intense. Two spiders reached the top of the chest, and she brought the broom down with a thump that rattled the doors. She raised the broom wildly again, and the blow had either killed or severely stunned the spiders. Two more reached the top, and again the broom came down with amazing force from such a small woman.

He peered behind the chest. No more spiders. They all lay motionless atop the mess chest. He took the shoe and pounded them to black pulps. He held out his hand. "Give me the broom a minute."

For a second he thought she wouldn't relinquish it. "They're all dead," he said. "I just want to clean out the web. I don't want to get it all over my hand when I move the chest."

She nodded and handed him the broom. "You're sure they're all dead?" she asked in a quavering voice.

He laughed. "After that attack, how could they survive? You've mastered the art of death by broom, but I flattened them to be sure."

She gave a laugh, but it was a shaky, unconvincing one, and he realized just how terrified she had been. He put an arm around her and hugged her. "You're really terrified of spiders, aren't you?"

"All my life. I would never even kill them at home, just run screaming for my father. But I knew these had to be eliminated for Ruthie to be safe." Her lips quirked in a slight smile. "Love conquers fear, I guess."

Love conquers fear. The words struck a chord in his heart. Was it fear that had been holding him back from allowing himself to fall in love with his wife? When he'd traveled West on the orphan train, he'd put up a high wall. He'd feared love would make him easily hurt. As he grew, that wall had served him well, but now it had started to crumble under Bessie's steadfast love and loyalty. What was the other verse? *"Perfect love casteth out fear."* He had to figure out how to allow God to create perfect love in his life.

⟳

Bessie had never had a man's attention the way she had that day. Jasper was so attentive and sweet all day. After they killed the spiders he helped her rearrange the furniture, and then he went to the quartermaster for some wool blankets. She stitched them together and made a rug for the parlor to cover the bare floors. The room looked so warm and cozy that she felt as though she had a real home now, a home of her own.

They baked oatmeal cookies together and played with Ruth in the afternoon. Ruthie enjoyed her first cookie immensely, and they had laughed at the expression on her face. Jasper asked Bessie to read from his book of Walt Whitman poetry, and they studied more about love from the Bible after Ruth went to bed for the evening. Jasper had built her a crib out of two crates that would suffice for a few months.

The candle burned down, and Bessie knew it was time for bed, but she was reluctant for the day to end. Tomorrow their life would resume as normal. Jasper would go back to work, and Eve would come again to help with the pile of laundry that waited. But today had been a day Bessie would not soon forget.

"I think I'll haul in some water for morning before we turn in."

How thoughtful of him. Bessie smiled, and he kissed her cheek.

"I'll be right back."

She watched him go out the back door with the pitcher. He left the back door open, and just before he came back in, a black shape flew in. A bird or a moth? She couldn't tell what it was, but it would have to be shooed back outside. Sighing, she got to her feet and went to fetch the broom. That ratty broom Jasper had made had come in handy today.

By the time she found the broom, the bird or whatever it was had managed to hide. Where had it gone?

"Another spider?"

She hadn't heard Jasper come back in. "No, a bird got in. I was going to shoo it out, but I don't know where it's gone."

Jasper helped her look for it, but neither one of them could see it.

"Let me get the lantern." Jasper went to the parlor and fetched the lantern. Its bright light illuminated the dark corners.

"There it is!" Bessie pointed to the corner near the fireplace in the parlor.

"I see it." Jasper approached the shadow on the ceiling. He touched the broom to it, and it took off flying, then dove directly at Bessie's head.

She ducked. "It's a bat!" She had seen them occasionally in the attic at home but had never had one fly directly at her. Once one had gotten trapped in Lenore's hair. She had to be revived with smelling salts.

Bessie covered her hair with her hands and cowered on the floor. Jasper chased the bat around and around the room. He fell over furniture and banged his shin against the doorway, but the bat still eluded him.

"Open the front and back doors, and I'll see if I can chase it out."

She didn't want to get up, so she crawled to the front door and swung it open. She ran outside, around to the back, and opened the back door. The door to the bedroom was shut, so Ruthie was safe. Bessie would stay outside until the thing was gone. She could hear Jasper whacking the broom as he tried to get the bat to fly out. Suddenly a black shape came zipping out the back door, and she screamed and cowered again.

"What is it, missus?" The soldier on guard duty appeared at her side almost immediately.

"Just a bat."

He shuddered and hurried away. She guessed she wasn't the only one who hated bats.

"It's gone," she called to Jasper. She closed the door behind her and went to the parlor to find him.

He appeared at the front door. His hair stuck up in spikes, his shirt had come untucked, and he looked wild eyed. She chuckled. The chuckle turned into a giggle and then full-blown laughter. Jasper stared at her, then his own chuckle started. It fed Bessie's mirth and, holding her stomach, she sat on the cot. She laughed so hard she cried.

"It's not that funny," Jasper protested between his own laughter. He dropped beside her and tickled her. "I'll give you something to laugh about."

He grabbed her ribs, and she shrieked. "No, I'm ticklish!"

"That's the whole point." He pulled her onto his lap and poked her a couple of more times until she begged for mercy.

"You don't deserve mercy," he pointed out. "You deserted me in my hour of need."

"It was only a bat. I thought you could handle it on your own." She laughed.

"I'll let you off this time, but don't let it happen again." He stopped tickling her but kept his arms around her.

"I hope we don't have a bat in here again. If we do, I can't promise anything." Her smile died at the tender expression in his eyes. She gravely searched his gaze and closed her eyes as his lips came down on hers.

"I don't want to sleep in the parlor anymore," he whispered. "What do you say to that? We'll take it slow, Bessie. I won't share your bed yet, just the room."

What did she say to that? Her heart beat wildly in her throat. She was suddenly terrified.

He kissed her again, and her terror melted. This was right, and God had joined them. It didn't matter if Jasper didn't love her. She had enough love for both of them. She smiled shyly and nodded.

Thirteen

Bessie hummed as she prepared a bottle for Ruth. Bessie felt love and contentment in their predictable routine. Jasper seemed happy too. Several times she had been tempted to tell him she loved him, but somehow the words always stuck in her throat. She wanted to hear him say those words first. Would she have to wait the rest of her life?

Ruth tugged on her skirt, and Bessie looked down. At seven months old, Ruth was trying to learn to crawl. She would get on her hands and knees and rock back and forth until she lunged forward. Bessie noticed Ruth had something in her mouth.

"Spit it out," Bessie commanded. She felt around and pulled out a sliver of wood. "Silly baby." She picked her up and kissed her silky neck, delighting in the soft warmth of the baby. It was hard to imagine how life could be better.

She heard the front door shut. That was odd. Eve usually came through the back door. "I'm in the kitchen," she called.

"It's me," Jasper said.

Her welcoming smile died when she saw the strain on his face. "What is it? What's wrong?"

He reached her in two strides and took her in his arms. "Sit down. I need to talk to you."

Numbly, she let him lead her to the table. Once she was seated, he knelt beside her and took her hand. "I have news–" He broke off, and his throat worked convulsively. "I don't know how to say this."

Terror seized her. Whatever it was, it was very bad. "Just tell me," she whispered.

He drew a deep breath. "The colonel called me into his office. It seems Ruthie's relatives have found out where she is, and they are laying claim to her."

In her worst nightmares she had imagined this. But how could anyone know where Ruthie was? And how could anyone ask her to give up her baby? "I'm the only mother she's ever known. I can't give her up."

Jasper struggled to control himself. He loved Ruth too. "There will be a hearing next week when all the evidence will be brought. But we must be prepared, Bessie. We may lose her."

"No!" Denial burst from her lips. "We'll take her East. Today, right now." She rose and paced wildly. "No one can find us there. They wouldn't even look. No one would care."

"What kind of life do you think our Ruthie would have back East with the prejudice she would have to endure?" Jasper said gently. "Can we do that to her to save ourselves now? Even living here with us will be difficult. When she is grown, she'll have trouble fitting in. We both know this."

"We would protect her from it," Bessie said piteously. "No one would dare say a word about the granddaughter of Benjamin Marsh Randall."

"Would your father claim her as his granddaughter?"

Bessie fell silent. No, he would not, nor her mother. They were as snobbish as any others in Boston. But how could anyone not love Ruthie?

Jasper took Bessie in his arms and stroked her hair. "We must be strong and pray for God's will to be done."

Did she want God's will? What if his will was that she give up her daughter? Could she do that? No, that couldn't be his will. He had to work it out. He just had to.

"Do you know who is claiming her?" Perhaps it was a grandparent or an aunt or uncle. In that case, perhaps her own claim would be stronger.

"Her father."

Bessie's heart sank. "You are the only father she knows!"

"I know." A world of heartbreak punctuated each word.

She clutched him. "You have to think of something, Jasper."

"There is nothing. We have to go to the hearing and present the strongest case we're able to make. We'll gather witnesses who will testify of our love for her and the care we've given. We will leave it in God's hands. His will be done."

His will be done. The words sounded final and frightening. She tried to pray, but the words wouldn't come. Was it only moments ago she had been reflecting on how very blessed and fortunate she was? Tears stung her eyes.

Jasper pressed his lips against her forehead. "We'll get through this, Bessie. Somehow, we'll get through this."

When he left her she tried to think, to plan, but she was too numb. Tears finally fell, and when Eve came, Bessie was sitting at the table sobbing.

Eve shut the door behind her. "Bessie, what is wrong?"

At the concern in her friend's voice, the tears began again. "Ruthie's father is laying claim to her."

Eve was silent. "I feared this would happen. It has become common knowledge that a white woman at Fort Bowie found a baby in the desert and adopted her. Children are precious to the Navajo."

"We need people who will testify that we love her and have cared well for her. Would you be our advocate?"

"Of course, my friend. And I know Ben will also say how he found Ruthie and how your Jasper was searching for her." She laid a hand on Bessie's shoulder. "Do not despair. Our God is in control of this. We will pray for his will."

"But what if his will is to take Ruthie from us?"

"Then that is what is best for Ruthie."

Bessie couldn't accept that. What was best for Ruthie, for all of them, was for their family to stay together.

The week dragged by. Bessie spent every moment with Ruth

and drank in every expression of delight, every moment of joy. It was a bittersweet time that made her appreciate her daughter even more.

A pall seemed to hang over the fort too. The men loved the baby, and they stopped by at odd times to offer their help if there was anything they could do. Bessie or Jasper thanked them and even asked one or two to testify on their behalf. Rooster would testify, as would the colonel.

The day of the hearing finally arrived. Bessie dressed carefully in her best dress. The blue fabric brought out the color of her gray eyes. She wanted to look competent enough to care for the needs of a child. Jasper looked splendid in his freshly brushed uniform, but his eyes were sober. She knew hers were full of fear. She had seen it in the mirror when she brushed her hair.

Jasper took the baby, then helped Bessie up onto the buckboard. He gave Ruth to her, then climbed up beside her. A group of twelve soldiers escorted them out of the fort. The Indian agent's office was about five miles away.

If the circumstances had been different, Bessie would have enjoyed her first excursion outside the confines of Fort Bowie in six months. Just to see different cactus and scrub was a treat. They bounced along the rutted track, and she tried to remember all she wanted to say. She must not lose her temper or her composure. She had to convince them that the baby would be better with her.

She snuggled Ruthie close and tried not to imagine the return trip if she had to give her up. It couldn't happen. There was no way any man would require Ruth to return to a father she had never known.

All too soon they stopped in front of the agent's quarters, a square adobe structure with several Indians milling around. Bessie caught sight of Eve and raised her hand in greeting. The man beside her must be Ben. They both responded with lopsided smiles.

Jasper took the baby and helped Bessie down from the buckboard. She claimed Ruth from him and followed him inside. Several Indians were inside as well as a man in his fifties with graying hair and a handlebar mustache.

"McCloskey, the Indian agent," Jasper whispered.

He looked like a reasonable man. Bessie sent him a tiny smile, which he returned. She didn't have many feminine wiles, but she intended to use what few she had to keep her baby.

Glancing around the room, she was surprised to see Black Will, the young Navajo who had taught the soldiers construction techniques. He stood with a group of three other Navajo men and two women. One of the women, a beautiful young woman of about twenty-five, sent her a glare. The other, an older woman with graying hair, nodded politely in her direction.

"I think we're all here now," McCloskey said ponderously. "Please be seated, all of you, until you are called to tell your side of the story. Let's hear from the man laying claim to the child."

One of the young men with Black Will stepped up. "I am called Thomas by the white man. The child is mine." He was tall and well built with a self-confidence unusual in an Indian.

His quiet, confident demeanor caused Bessie's heart to sink. She should have known the man who would father a darling like Ruth would be someone with whom to reckon.

"What proof do you have?"

"I have those who will testify where the child was found as well as the family birthmark she carries on the inside of her knee. It matches the one on mine. My mother is here to swear that the woman was my wife, and that we were legally wed according to our laws and lived together as man and wife."

Bessie looked him over. *How did he come to speak such perfect English?*

"Bring forward your witnesses."

His mother testified first of her son's marriage and his wife and the love they shared. She told of their joy when they found they would have a child.

"How did the mother come to give birth in the desert?" Agent McCloskey asked.

"She was on her way to gather supplies and was set upon by Apaches. They took her wagon and left her in the desert. The shock brought on her labor," Thomas explained quietly.

"How do you know this?"

"My brother found my wagon and persuaded the thief to tell the story." He smiled grimly as he gestured to Black Will. "Black Will is my brother."

The agent cleared his throat gruffly. "I see."

Then the Navajo who had been their guide told how the baby

had been found by Jasper and Bessie. He had seen the dead woman with his own eyes and testified as to the clothing she had been wearing. He had taken the grieving husband to her grave, and he had identified the clothing as belonging to his wife. "My brother saw the child's birthmark with his own eyes."

The chips were stacking up against them. Bessie could feel the panic rising. When did she get to plead for her daughter?

Abruptly the agent turned to Jasper. "Have you anything to add to this, Lieutenant? The evidence seems pretty clear."

Jasper stood and cleared his throat. "Yes, sir. We freely admit we found Ruth. We have loved and cared for her these seven months as if she were our own child. Indeed, we feel she is our own child. We could not love her more if she were our own flesh and blood. We ask you to think of her welfare also. We can give her many advantages and much love. We have several witnesses who can testify that we have given her excellent care."

Agent McCloskey waved his hand. "That won't be necessary, Lieutenant. I'm sure you and your wife have been good caretakers. But this child belongs to her father, and since you are not disputing that fact, I have no choice but to order her to be given back to him."

"No!" Bessie sprang to her feet. "You can't. Think of Ruth. We're the only parents she knows. She's too young to understand. Please, you must not do this." She began to weep, wringing her hands. How could she make them understand? She turned imploring eyes to the young father. She thought she saw compassion in his eyes, and she took a step toward him.

Jasper put a restraining hand on her arm. "Bessie, don't. It's no use."

She shook off his hand. "I can't let them take her. Please, Jasper." She turned back to the agent. "Please don't do this, sir. She's our baby. We love her so much." Sobs wracked her body, and she held Ruth close.

"I'm sorry, ma'am. I have no choice." He turned back to Thomas and his family. "You may take the child."

Bessie whirled and would have fled with Ruth, but Jasper stopped her. Thomas walked slowly toward them, then turned back and faced agent McCloskey. "I will give Lieutenant Mendenhall and his wife two days to say their good-byes to my daughter and prepare for the separation. I do not wish to cause them any more harm. I am grateful for their care of my daughter." His eyes were full of compassion when he faced them. "I will come for her in two days. Please have her ready."

He walked away, and Jasper took Bessie's arm and half carried her to the waiting buckboard. She was dazed. This couldn't be happening. She wanted Ruthie to know the Lord, to be taught the Bible. Her precious baby was going into spiritual darkness.

She fought the feeling of light-headedness and stumbled along as best as she could. She encountered the shocked faces of her friends as she passed. Eve moved as if to go to her, but Ben restrained her.

Jasper helped her into the buckboard and climbed up beside her. They were silent with shock and sorrow as the buckboard lurched along. Bessie stole a glance at her husband. His jaw was set, and his face was white.

"How could he do this, Jasper? I don't understand how this could happen."

"I feared the worst. I think the agent felt he had to keep the Indians appeased. We have enough trouble with the Apache without riling the Navajo. And as her father, Thomas does have a right to her. Think how we would feel in his place."

Bessie shook her head. "Let's just go, Jasper. Just keep driving until we reach the stage stop. We'll go to California or back to Fort Bridger. Somewhere they'll never find us."

"The army would find me, Bessie. I would be a deserter."

She had forgotten that. But there must be somewhere they could go. "What are we going to do?"

He heaved a sigh. "We have no choice, Bessie. We must give Ruthie back to her father."

She was shaking her head before he even finished. "You've never been a quitter, Jasper. Why are you giving up now? We can't give her back. We just can't."

He stopped the buckboard and turned to face her. "You have to stop this, Bessie. We have no choice. None. I would give anything if we could keep her with us. But the fact is that she is that man's daughter, the child of his own body. What if your true child had been lost to you and you found she was alive and living with another family? Would you want her back?"

She stared at him. She would want her child back. Could she

blame Ruth's father for wanting what any father would desire? Hopeless tears leaked from her eyes, and she buried her face in her hands.

They finished the trip in silence. Bessie wished she could just die. How was she to face that man when he came to her door? How could she hand Ruthie into his arms? She closed her eyes and moaned.

When they reached their quarters, Jasper helped her down. "I need to report the decision to the colonel. I'll be in shortly." He hugged her gently and hurried across the parade ground.

She carried Ruth inside and laid the sleeping child in her crib. Soon that crib would be empty. Soon her arms would be even emptier. She dropped onto the cot in the living room and buried her head in her hands. She couldn't bear it. Why did God allow something like this to happen? Could this really be his will? She couldn't begin to think of any way this could be the right thing. Was it only her own will that made her so certain?

Neither one of them could eat supper. Jasper just picked at his stew, and Bessie didn't even try to eat. She felt if a single morsel passed her lips, she would throw up. Ruthie was particularly adorable that evening. She giggled and pulled on Jasper's pant leg. She blew bubbles at Bessie and gurgled. Every time she babbled what sounded like Mama or Dada, they winced. It was all Bessie could do to keep her composure throughout the evening.

The next two days were bittersweet. The fort commander gave Jasper the time off to spend with his family. They took Ruth for walks, gathered the clothes Bessie had so lovingly made, and spent time just holding the baby. Bessie told her she was going for a nice visit with her daddy, but that they would always love her.

The knock on the door came too soon. Bessie held Ruth's soft body against hers and trembled. She couldn't do it. Praying for strength, she nodded to Jasper to open the door. His face white, he walked to the door and opened it. Thomas and his mother stood on the stoop.

"Come in," Jasper said. "The baby is ready, but I can't say we are."

The Navajos did not answer that comment but stepped inside. Ruth's grandmother smiled at the baby, then her grave eyes met Bessie's.

"Again, I thank you for all you have done for my daughter." Thomas approached Bessie with Ruth in her arms and spoke softly to her in Navajo.

Ruth buried her face against Bessie and didn't look at him. Bessie tightened her arms around her, and tears spilled from her eyes. "Please don't do this," she begged softly.

Thomas's gaze met hers. "She is my daughter. I have searched for her for seven months. Would you deny me the right to raise her in the traditions of her people? What can you give her that I cannot? Love? I love her more than you know. Money? I have my own ranch and am not a poor man. I have enough to see to her needs."

"She loves us," Bessie whispered. "Can't you see that? We are her parents now. I don't mean to hurt you, but she doesn't know you."

"She will learn. It will be hard for a few days, but she is just a baby. She will adjust. My mother and sister look forward to teaching her." There was no compromise in his eyes. She could sense his compassion, but she knew he would not change his mind. He would take Ruth, walk through the front door, and she would never see her again.

"Could I visit her?" She found it almost impossible to speak past the tears in her throat.

He hesitated. "Perhaps someday. But not now. She needs time to accept us and for us to accept her. She will be happy with us. She would never be truly accepted in your world. I think you know this in your heart."

She tightened her arms around Ruth and backed away a step. Tears shimmered in Jasper's eyes as he came toward her and stood beside her.

Thomas held out his arms. "My daughter, please."

Bessie searched his eyes and then looked at Jasper. The pain she saw reflected there almost broke her composure totally. She buried her nose in Ruth's neck and inhaled her baby scent for the last time.

Jasper bent his head and kissed Ruth's cheek. "Take her quickly," he muttered brokenly.

Bessie thrust the baby into her father's arms, and then she turned and ran from the room.

Fourteen

The bright sun shone most of the time in Arizona Territory, but Jasper knew that Bessie never saw it for days. A dark cloud of despair seemed to have wrapped itself around her heart and colored everything she said and did. Jasper was helpless to penetrate her depression. He missed her gentle smiles and thoughtful gestures. He didn't recognize this hollow-eyed stranger who never laughed.

He was dealing with his own grief too. The house echoed with memories of Ruthie—her laughter, her smiling eyes, and childish voice. How would they ever find their way out of this maze of despair? Perhaps if he were a real husband to her and there was the possibility of a child, Bessie could throw off this depression. But now was not the time to discuss that subject.

He stopped Eve on her way to his house nearly two weeks after Ruth was returned to her father. "What am I to do about Bessie? Does she talk to you at all?"

Eve's eyes were filled with grief. "She does not speak. It is as if the laughing part has died."

Jasper raked a hand through his hair. "The evenings are like sitting alone. She stares into space and only answers my questions when she has no choice."

Eve nodded. "Could she go home for a visit? Perhaps it would help her to see her own people."

His heart sank. He hated to think about being without her. But the woman sharing his home was not the Bessie he had come to admire and love. And he did love her. He knew that now when she had left him in spirit. Several times he had tried to tell her, but the words died before they were born.

He thanked Eve, and with lagging steps he went to check on a ticket. This was the only thing he could think to do. Once he checked the stage schedule and the cost of a ticket, he headed back across the parade ground to tell Bessie.

❧

Bessie didn't bother to give Eve any instructions. Her friend knew the house as well as she did. Besides, none of it seemed very important. Their quarters could have been covered in dust and cobwebs, and she wouldn't have noticed. What reason did she have to keep it clean? No precious baby would crawl across its floors . . . no pudgy fingers would reach to put stray dirt into her mouth.

She thought of Boston. The emerald lawns and trees, the parties and laughter. What would Jasper say if she told him she wanted to go home? She longed for green grass, for parties to take her mind off her loss. She wanted to share with her family what a lovely child Ruthie was. Surely they would understand her loss if she told them in person, wouldn't they? She wanted to get away from this house filled with memories of her smiling baby.

If Lenore was no longer seeing Richard, perhaps Bessie should step aside and let Jasper have the woman he really wanted. Although it would mean her own ruin, Bessie would have some satisfaction in seeing another's happiness. What did it matter if her reputation was in tatters now? Her daughter was gone.

She stared at the bright spot of sunshine on the kitchen floor. Why did the sun continue to rise each day when in her heart she felt only darkness?

She knew Jasper was concerned for her. He stared at her when he thought she wasn't looking. First he was saddled with a wife he didn't know, then he was left with this shell. And that's how she felt. A shell. All the joy and happiness had fled from her spirit. Jasper deserved better.

She thought she still loved him, but any emotion was hidden deep inside. It hurt too much to care. If she went away, he would soon forget her.

The front door banged, and she jumped. Jasper smiled at her anxiously.

"What are you doing home? You just left."

He took her hands in his. "How would you like to go home, to Boston, for a while?"

How had he known? She stared at him silently. She had been nothing like a wife to him lately. Though she knew it, she couldn't help herself, couldn't shake the grief that hung over her like a shroud.

He rushed on as if he thought he had to convince her. "I've checked on stage tickets, and you could leave tomorrow or Friday. You could stay as long as you like, get caught up on all the news with your sister. She would be delighted to see you. The autumn balls will be in full swing soon."

"I'll go. I have been thinking about it."

His face lit up and he hugged her. Her heart clenched with pain. Had he been looking for an excuse to send her home all this time? "I want to go tomorrow."

His smile dimmed, but he nodded and kissed her forehead. "I'll buy the ticket."

Eve stared at her from the kitchen where she had begun the laundry. "I will pack your valise."

"I'd rather do it," Bessie said. "I know what I want to take." She would take everything important just in case she never returned.

Eve nodded and returned to her chores. Bessie went to the bedroom to pack. The sooner she was gone from this house of painful memories, the better.

❧

While standing at the stage stop the next day, Bessie felt as though she were in a cocoon of cotton—she couldn't feel anything. No pain, no joy, no feelings of any kind. She hugged Jasper and allowed him to kiss her, but her heart felt like a block of wood in her chest. His blue eyes stared at her worriedly, then he helped her aboard the stage. Did he suspect she might not return?

"Write when you arrive safely."

"I will."

He looked as though he had more he wanted to say, but in the end, he shut the stage door and stepped away. She lifted a gloved hand and waved at him gravely, then she fixed her gaze straight ahead. She wouldn't allow herself to feel regret.

The days aboard the stagecoach were an ordeal, but Bessie loved the train. The train whistle blew, and Boston was just ahead. She felt the most excitement she had felt since before Ruthie had been ripped from her. Leaning out the train window, she breathed in the moist air. How she had missed the green grass and leafy trees!

When Jasper had kissed her at the stage stop, she had tried to tell him she wouldn't be back, but the words wouldn't come. Had that been relief on his face when he waved good-bye?

The train jerked to a halt, and she gathered her valise and reticule. She tied her bonnet firmly under her chin, then pushed her way through the throng and looked anxiously around for a familiar face.

"Bessie!"

She whirled around and Lenore hurtled toward her at a most

unladylike pace. Behind her came her parents. "Lenore." Tears pricked her eyes, and she flung herself into her sister's embrace. Her parents arrived, and she hugged them.

"Let me look at you." Her father held her at arm's length. "What are these dark circles? Isn't that new husband taking care of you?"

She bristled at the criticism of Jasper. "Of course he is. It's just been a long trip."

Her father snorted. "I thought you said you wanted adventure." He linked his arm with hers. Her mother looped her arm through Bessie's other elbow, and they strolled toward the waiting carriage. She knew they looked the picture of a happy, prosperous family. Appearances were so important to her parents.

Lenore kept up a steady stream of comments as she followed them. "Your letters said you were bitten by a rattlesnake. Do you have a scar? What's it like living in a place that hot? Is it true there is no green grass?"

Bessie laughed and was surprised at the sound. She had thought she would never laugh again. This trip had been a good idea.

❧

Her room looked just the same. Her clothes were still in the wardrobe, and her extra shoes lined the end of her bed. Her room was the same, but why did it all feel so different? She gazed at her reflection in the mirrored dresser. Her appearance was unaltered, but she knew she was not the same young woman who had stood there eight months before. It was like trying to fit into a dress a size too small. Not impossible, but not comfortable either.

Lenore pecked on the door. "Dinner, Bessie. Emma made your favorite. Fried chicken."

She grabbed her shawl and joined her sister in the hall. Their parents were already seated at the dining room table. Her father rose politely until his daughters were seated, then he rang for Emma to serve the meal.

As they ate, Bessie was conscious of the stares the three of them sent her way when they thought she wasn't looking. She knew the inquisition would begin after dinner. When the last plates were cleared away, her mother suggested they retire to the game room. Bessie laid down her napkin and followed her family.

"You look terrible, Bessie. I want to know what's been going on out there in the desert. Is your husband kind?"

"Oh, Mother, of course he is. Jasper is the sweetest, kindest man I've ever met." Bessie was shocked they would think anything different. She had written them of her husband's many fine qualities.

"Your sister finally confessed her part in your hasty marriage," her father began ponderously. "I must say your mother and I were shocked you didn't confide the truth to us."

"I wanted to go, Father."

He waved his large hand. "That is beside the point. Your sister acted irresponsibly, and so did you."

Bessie couldn't argue with that. She glanced at Lenore, but her sister avoided her gaze.

"Have you left your husband?"

How had they guessed? She took a deep breath. "I haven't decided. Don't think it's Jasper's fault." She pressed her hands together. "We lost the child we'd adopted, and I'm afraid I haven't dealt well with the loss."

Her father frowned, and Lenore leaned forward, her eyes sparkling. Was she still yearning after Jasper?

"Whose child was it?" Her mother sounded bewildered.

"An Indian child, Mother." Bessie burst into tears and sobbed out the story of Ruthie.

Her mother's face pursed in disapproval. "You should have searched for the child's parents immediately, Bessie, and you would not have gotten attached to her."

She knew they would react this way. Why had she tried to deceive herself? She straightened her shoulders and got to her feet. "I'm tired. May I be excused?"

Her father's expression darkened, but he nodded curtly. "We will discuss this tomorrow."

As Bessie fled for the sanctuary of her room, she heard Lenore demanding to know what she intended to do. Bessie shut the door behind her and threw herself across the bed. Lenore wanted Jasper. Bessie had seen Lenore's acquisitive expression when she heard Bessie might be annulling the marriage. But hearing her father ask the question had made Bessie realize how impossible the very thought of it was.

She didn't belong here. This large brick structure with fine furniture and more room than they knew what to do with was no longer her home. Her home was an adobe three-room building with a cot for a sofa and a handmade kitchen table. Jasper was her family. She belonged with her husband.

Her parents would tell her they loved her, but real love was what Jasper had been showing her for months. He might not have said the words, but he told her with his actions, just like the Bible said he should. She saw his love in the way he saw to her needs— giving of his money and possessions willingly, hauling wood so she wouldn't have to carry it—his kind words, and tender care. All the little things he did shouted his regard. Why had she doubted?

She had been hurt and confused, but now she was on the verge of a huge mistake. She thanked God he had guarded her from herself. What would Jasper say when she got home? Would he even expect to see her again? Had he realized the finality of her good-bye?

She looked up at the knock on the door.

"May I come in, Bessie?" Her sister's voice was soft as though she feared their father would hear.

Bessie opened the door. "I'm not giving up Jasper. You can come in, but if you're here to try to convince me to leave him, you're wasting your breath."

Lenore stared at her and shook her head. She brushed past her and shut the door. "I don't want your Jasper, Bessie. You should know better. I can see you love him. All I've ever wanted was for you to be happy."

Bessie searched her sister's eyes and nodded. What had she been thinking? Lenore was sometimes irresponsible and thoughtless, but she would never deliberately harm her.

"I just want to hear about the West. Do you think I could come for a visit? My hopes for marriage here have not materialized. I'm so sick of Boston society, of Father's determination to find me a man of substance." She shook her head. "I don't care about money. I want a husband who is a real man, not my father's paid lackey." Her eyes gleamed. "I've thought about writing and asking, but I was afraid you'd say no. But now that you're here and I can tell you I have no designs on your husband, maybe you'll take pity on me."

Bessie laughed. She felt as though a huge weight had been lifted from her shoulders. Lenore didn't want Jasper. Her smile faded. What if he still yearned for her? The last thing she needed was for Jasper to be around Lenore. The comparison would be devastating to her marriage. "Are you sure you don't still care for Jasper? You wrote to him even after I went West."

A guilty expression raced across her sister's face. "Yes, I did. I'm surprised he told you."

"He didn't. I saw the letter."

"Did you read it?" Lenore's question was casual. Too casual.

"No. I couldn't betray Jasper like that." She frowned at the relief on Lenore's face.

Her sister got to her feet. "I must get to bed," she said airily. "Don't worry about the letter, Bessie. It meant nothing. Not to me or to Jasper."

Her eyes narrowed, Bessie watched her sister's hurried departure. What had been in the letter?

The days were lonely for Jasper without Bessie, and the nights
even lonelier. The little house echoed. The laundry was neatly
folded and put away and the house was spotless after Eve's visits,
but it lacked Bessie's touch. Several times Jasper had been tempted
to send her a letter begging her to come home, but he managed to
restrain himself. He wanted the old Bessie back, and if he forced
her hand, he feared he would never see his laughing wife again,
just her empty shell.

October was drawing to a close. Soon the welcome mon-
soon would arrive. Would she be home for Thanksgiving, for
Christmas? Would she come home at all? He forced himself to
face the possibility that she might not. Her good-bye had seemed
so final. As she had clung to him with a strange desperation, she
searched his eyes with her grave gaze, as though imprinting his
likeness on her mind. Why had he never realized before just how
precious she was to him? Was it too late to tell her?

He thought of Ruthie. How was she getting along with her
father? He was tempted to ask Black Will several times, but he didn't
want to speak with the man who had been responsible for this turn
of events. He was being unfair. After all, Black Will was Ruthie's
uncle, but Jasper couldn't seem to rid himself of the animosity.

It was late when he let himself in the house. How odd. The lamp in the bedroom was lit. Frowning, he walked through the parlor and kitchen and pushed open the bedroom door.

Bessie lay in the bed fast asleep. His mouth gaped. She must have come in on the stage late this afternoon. He had heard the normal stage commotion, but he hadn't thought anything about it. She couldn't have been in Boston longer than a few days. What had caused her to come back so quickly? He wished he could believe it was because she missed him.

Relief flooded him. If she hadn't come soon, he would have been compelled to go after her. In spite of the strange circumstances of their marriage, Bessie was his wife.

He knelt by the bed and just drank in the sight of her. Her light-brown hair spread over the pillow, and he buried his face in it. He kissed her gently, but she didn't awaken, and he saw the shadows of exhaustion under her eyes. What a grueling trip she had to have endured. He ran his fingers over her lower lip and kissed her.

"Bessie," he said softly.

She opened her eyes and stared at him. Then she smiled and opened her arms.

Jasper gathered her close. "Don't ever leave me again, Bessie. You're all I have. We can have a baby together and build our family from tonight forward." He kissed her gently at first and then with mounting passion. "I love the way your hair smells as fresh as sunshine, the way you tilt your head when you smile," he muttered against her neck. "Promise you'll never leave me again."

"I promise," Bessie whispered. Then she moved over for him to join her in their bed.

Fifteen

The smell of coffee awakened Bessie. For just a moment she forgot where she was. Then she smelled the scent of sage wafting through the open window and saw the bathtub hanging on the wall. She smiled and stretched. She was home.

She heard Jasper moving around the kitchen, and she got up and quickly dressed. He whistled as he banged the coffeepot back down on the stove.

She pinched some color into her cheeks and opened the bedroom door. Everything had changed last night. She felt shy at the thought of facing him this morning.

He turned at the sound and grinned. "Couldn't stand a place with no snakes or spiders, huh?"

She smiled. "And no bats." She drank in the sight of him with his silly grin and tender eyes.

"I missed you," he said softly.

"I knew as soon as I arrived in Boston that I had made a mistake. There's nothing left back there for me."

"And here you have sagebrush and sand, rattlesnakes and scorpions. What more could you want?"

"Ruthie," she said without thinking.

His mirth faded. "I know."

"Have you heard anything about her at all?"

He looked away and expelled a heavy sigh.

"Tell me!" She panicked at the look of resignation on his face.

"It's nothing bad. It's just—" He broke off and sighed again. "I'm not sure it's the best thing for either of us, but her uncle said we would be permitted to visit her."

Joy flooded her heart. To see her baby again, to touch her. "When?" she asked eagerly.

"Whenever you want. The family is still in the area right now. They will be leaving next week to go back north."

"Can we go today?" She wanted to go right now, this minute. She couldn't wait to feel Ruthie's chubby arms around her neck, to smell the sweet baby scent of her.

"I've already asked for the day off."

"Let me comb my hair." She hurried to the bedroom, brushed her hair, and put it up. She picked up her bonnet and rushed toward the front door, but Jasper stopped her. "You must eat something, Bessie. You're white with fatigue."

"I'm not hungry." She smiled. "Let's just go. I can eat later." But when she swayed, she realized he might be right. When had she eaten last? She hadn't been able to force down much at the stage stops.

Jasper guided her to a seat and nudged her down. "You have to take care of yourself. You're all I have."

Bessie was touched at his admission. She searched his tender gaze. "All right. I'll have some bread and jam. That coffee smells wonderful too." She started to get up, but he shook his head firmly.

"I'll get it. You look like a stiff wind would blow you over. I don't think much of the care your family has given you."

She didn't tell him they had said the same thing about him. "How's Eve?"

"She's taken good care of the house, as you can see. She'll be glad you're back."

Why were they talking about such mundane things? Why didn't he sweep her into his arms and tell her never to leave again? Had he really missed her? What had last night meant to him? The questions stuck in her throat.

"I'll get the buckboard while you finish your breakfast."

By the time she was done, he was back. "Ready?"

She took a last gulp of coffee. "Ready."

Several of the soldiers waved and welcomed her home. The buckboard bounced over the ruts and scrub, and she clung to Jasper's arm to keep from being thrown from the seat. The scent of creosote and sage was like a tonic. How good it was to be home!

They headed toward the small encampment west of the fort. Several ramshackle adobe buildings squatted amid the cactus and yucca. She saw half-clothed children playing in the dirt with several dogs, and her heart sank. Was this the kind of life her Ruthie would have?

Jasper stopped the buckboard at the first building and asked where he might find Thomas. The somber woman pointed to the last building in the row. He tipped his hat, and they went on. The building looked deserted, and Bessie frowned. What if the family had already left? Jasper helped her down, and they went to the door.

Bessie felt as though she could barely breathe. The door finally opened, and Thomas's mother stared at them impassively.

"We've come to see Ruth," Jasper said.

The woman motioned them inside. It took several moments for Bessie's eyes to adjust to the dim interior, then she saw Ruthie lying on a blanket. The baby slept with her thumb corked in her mouth as usual. She was clean, her hair neatly plaited in tiny braids.

Bessie went onto her knees with a soft cry. Ruthie opened her eyes and stared at her. Her mouth puckered, and she sought her grandmother's face.

Her grandmother went to her with soft clucking sounds of comfort, and the little girl held up her arms. She stared soberly at Bessie and Jasper from the sanctuary of her grandmother's arms.

Bessie thought her heart would break. How could Ruthie have forgotten them so quickly? It had only been six weeks. "Hello, darling." She touched her soft hair, then patted her cheek. "Have you forgotten me?"

"Ma-ma-ma," Ruthie chanted. She reached up a chubby hand and grasped an escaping tendril of Bessie's hair.

Tears of relief flooded Bessie's eyes. Perhaps she hadn't forgotten them totally. Did she think they had deserted her? Bessie touched her soft cheek again, so engrossed in the baby, she didn't hear Thomas come in until he spoke.

"You have come."

She and Jasper both turned. Thomas stood in the doorway, his feet apart, his arms crossed on his chest.

He gave Ruth a fond gaze. "You see she has adjusted well. I wanted to set your minds at ease before we go home."

"She looks happy," Bessie said grudgingly. "She obviously loves her grandmother."

Thomas nodded. "She cried the first day, but then no longer. This will be the last time we meet. I wished you to see she was well. You love her and saved her from death. Now you can rest knowing she will be happy."

"Where are you going?" Jasper asked.

"Home to my ranch, then wherever the Lord leads."

Bessie stared at him in shock. What did he mean? Her heart pounded in sudden hope. Her worst nightmare had been that Ruthie was going into spiritual darkness.

He smiled at her expression. "I was raised by missionaries near the Colorado border. The Lord called me as his own when I was ten years old. I will do my best to raise my daughter in the ways of Jesus as we travel among my people to tell them of his love."

She gave Thomas her hand. "I can go now. I was wrong to question God's purposes. My faith was small. May God go with you."

He took her hand and pressed her fingers gently. "You allowed the Lord to work a miracle through you. I will tell Ruth of the woman with the eyes of love who saved her from the desert. Your reward will be great in heaven."

Tears streamed from her eyes at his words. Had God truly used her? Was there some greater purpose in these events? Only God knew, but Bessie thanked him for allowing her to have the joy of knowing Ruthie just those few short months.

Jasper put an arm around her and led her from the shanty. They both took one long, last look at Ruth. She stared at them and then smiled at her grandmother.

"Come, Bessie," Jasper said softly. "There's no need for us here."

Bessie's arms were empty, but her heart was full as they rode home. She had been so foolish to doubt God's provision and to question his will. She cast a sidelong glance at Jasper. The relief was evident on his face too.

❧

Although she still missed the baby, after several weeks Bessie was able to finally let go in her heart. She would accept God's will. The walls came tumbling down in her relationship with Jasper, too, now that they were truly man and wife—more than just in name. The tender light in her husband's eyes made her forget the disappointment she had seen there the day they met. Then something would remind her of Lenore, and she would still wonder how he would feel when he met her sister for the first time. They were certain to meet someday.

"I'll be gone all day," Jasper told her one morning over breakfast. "We have a lead about Cochise's whereabouts. There's a dance at the officer's quarters tonight. I'll make sure I'm back to take my best girl out on the town. Such as it is." He grinned at his own joke.

"I'll save every dance for you."

"We can eat at the mess hall tonight." He kissed her good-bye, and she got up to wash the dishes. A wave of nausea struck her, and she rushed to the bedroom for the chamber pot. She vomited and sat back weakly. What was wrong with her? She felt so light-headed.

A sense of unease seized her, and she went to the kitchen and looked at the cloth calendar hanging on the wall. Counting back she smiled incredulously. Today was her birthday, and she had forgotten all about it. If what she suspected were true, the Lord had presented them with the most perfect gift she could imagine.

Doctor Richter confirmed her suspicions. "You'll probably deliver in late July. I want you to get plenty of rest. You don't look well. Eve will be glad to come more often, I'm sure."

In a daze of joy she hurried back home. For a moment she almost felt guilty. No other child could replace Ruthie. Bessie would always love her, but God had seen fit to fill the hole in her heart. She hoped this would heal Jasper's heart as much as it did hers. He would be a wonderful father to this baby.

Her heart full of hope, she sat on the cot and waited for Jasper to come home. She would wait until after supper to tell him. The joy of savoring his anticipated reaction was sweet. A baby! It was almost beyond belief.

When Jasper came through the front door, she was still smiling. She stood and he put his arm around her.

"My sweet Bessie." He kissed her. "I missed seeing your smile today. You hungry?"

"Starved."

He chuckled. "I think it's beans and salt pork."

She smiled and gave a small shrug. "At least I don't have to cook it."

He held her hand as they crossed the parade ground. When they entered the mess hall, a rousing cheer went up.

"Happy birthday, Bessie!" the assembled soldiers shouted.

"Bessie!"

She turned. Was that Lenore's voice?

Her sister beamed at her. "Surprised?"

As they hugged each other the gentle fragrance of Lenore's lilac sachet slipped up Bessie's nose. "I'm speechless."

Lenore giggled. "I wrote Jasper months ago to plan this."

The hall was decorated with crudely painted signs, and a birthday cake sat on a center table surrounded with packages. Confetti, obviously hand cut from old newspapers, showered over her. Beaming with pride Jasper led her to the table and had her open her gifts.

Rooster gave her a small leather-bound diary. "It was my

mother's. I can't read, so I'll never use it. It would make me right proud to know you was writing in it."

Some gifts were homemade, like Private Bechtol's gift of a small dulcimer. Bessie was overwhelmed at the show of love.

"There's no gift here from me," Jasper whispered. "I'll give it to you at home later."

What could it be? Whatever it was, her gift to him would be even more joyous. She smiled at the thought.

"What's that smile about?" he asked while he spun her around the room when the band started playing.

"I'll tell you later."

Jasper refused to let any other soldier cut in, but the high-spirited men didn't care. They partnered Lenore when they could and danced with each other when they couldn't.

Bessie was exhausted by the time Jasper led her and Lenore back across the dark parade ground. He lit the lantern on the mess chest, while Bessie dropped onto the cot in the parlor.

"I'm just exhausted," Lenore said. "Can I go to bed? We can talk more tomorrow."

"Do you mind sleeping out here?"

"Of course not."

"See you in the morning." Bessie rose and followed Jasper to their bedroom and shut the door behind them.

"My feet hurt," she moaned. "You stepped on them twice."

He grinned and slipped her feet out of her boots. "Let me rub them. I never claimed to be a dancer."

She sighed at the touch of his strong fingers on her sore feet. She gazed at his bent head and savored the news she was about to tell him. They would be a true family now. Nothing could part them.

"Better?"

"Much." She tucked her bare feet under her skirt and smiled at him. "I have a present for you."

He cocked a quizzical eyebrow. "It's *your* birthday."

"That reminds me. How long have you been planning this party? I don't even know when your birthday is."

"Lenore and I planned it months ago." He set the lantern on the floor and pulled a letter out of his pocket. Bessie recognized it immediately. It was the letter from Lenore. "She wrote me shortly after you arrived to apologize for her deceit. She wanted me to know what a wonderful wife you would make and told me all kinds of things about you—your birthday, how much you love cats, the way you care for other people, the fact that you hate onions." He grinned. "She admitted you didn't know how to cook, but assured me you would soon learn."

Bessie's face flamed. Why had she assumed the worst? She met his gaze shamefacedly. "I saw the letter, but I didn't read it." She wanted no secrets between them any longer. "I thought you still loved Lenore and were writing to her." A weight rolled off her heart. She had longed to speak to him of this pain and uncertainty she felt.

His mouth dropped open. "How could you think that? We've

been studying about love, and I thought I was doing a good job of showing you I love you."

Did he just say he loved her? She smiled at him tremulously. "You never told me. I saw you cared. You said you loved things about me, but you never said you loved me. Lenore is the beauty, and I've lived so long in her shadow it's been hard to stop." Joy filled her heart at the love that shone on his face.

He shook his head. "My silly Bessie." He knelt beside her and took her hands. "I love you so much it hurts sometimes. I see your spirit, your gentleness, and the way you give of yourself to others, and it humbles me. You are more beautiful than any woman I've ever met."

"Not more beautiful than Lenore," she said sadly.

"You are more beautiful to me than any woman in the world. All Lenore is to me is your sister. I forgot Lenore when you insisted on keeping Ruthie. I saw your heart that day and couldn't help but love it. I know I don't deserve you, but with God's help, I'll try my best to make you happy."

She had been so blind. He was a man of integrity, a man who loved and honored her. He would be a wonderful father.

He pressed his lips against the palm of her hand. "I know it's been hard lately, Bessie, but we'll get through it. Someday God will bless us with more children, but until then we have each other."

Tears coursed down her cheeks. "I love you so much," she whispered. "I read your letters and knew you were the man I'd longed for all my life." She smoothed his hair back from his forehead and gazed into his blue eyes. "God has blessed us so much. More than you know."

"I know he has."

The tenderness in his eyes made her heart sing. Why had she allowed her insecurities to make her doubt him? She would never doubt him again. "You don't know about this blessing. We're going to have a baby." She almost hated to tell him. The anticipation had been sweet.

He stared at her then his eyes widened. "A baby? Us?" He whooped and stood, swinging her up into his arms.

He whirled around the room with her until she was dizzy and laughing. "Stop or I'll throw up. And besides, you'll have Lenore in here any minute."

He stopped immediately and stared into her eyes. "I thought I loved you before, but it was nothing compared to how I feel right now." He set her back onto the cot and put his hand in his pocket. Drawing out a small box, he opened it and took out a gold wedding band.

Bessie caught her breath at the sight of the ring. How did he know she had longed for a tangible sign of his love, a visible announcement to all that she belonged to him?

He knelt again and took her left hand. "You are my precious treasure, Bessie. I want you to wear this and always remember that I will never leave your side until God takes me home." He pronounced the words solemnly, his eyes full of promise and commitment. He slipped the ring on her finger, then pressed his lips to it and sealed it in place.

Bessie felt she finally saw his heart. He was a stranger no longer and never would be again. She was flesh of his flesh and bone of his bone. He opened his arms, and she went into them with an overwhelming joy in her heart. No matter where the Lord led, she knew her heart was safe with this man, her beloved husband.

Epilogue

Jasper looked up at the sound of a baby's cry. Pacing the kitchen floor, he waited for the doctor to announce whether he had a son or a daughter. He didn't care which it was as long as Bessie and the baby were safe and well. She hadn't cried out at all but had endured her labor with the same courage he had first loved about her. He heard a murmur, and then the baby cried again.

A few minutes later the door opened, and a very disheveled Doctor Richter motioned him in. Propped in the bed, Bessie smiled at him wearily. His gaze traveled over her anxiously. She was pale, but she seemed to be all right. Only then did he glance down to see the baby. His jaw dropped. Two babies. And they both had red hair.

Bessie chuckled at the expression on his face. "Do you want to hold Cassie or Charles first?"

Jasper laughed. Bessie's eyes met his, and she joined him in laughter. He knelt beside the bed and kissed his wife, his son, and his daughter. "God said he would give us blessings beyond all we could dream or imagine. I think this is what he meant."

Discussion Questions

1. How do you feel about the world placing so much emphasis on outward beauty?
2. What do you feel is the most important trait of inner beauty? What was Bessie's strongest trait?
3. Why do you think Lenore did what she did?
4. Arranged marriages were not unusual back then. Should Jasper have been as upset as he was?
5. Commitment meant something to Bessie. What would you have done in the same situation?
6. Was it right for the baby to be returned to her father, or should Bessie and Jasper have been allowed to keep her?
7. Bessie ran off to Boston. What woke her up to what was really important?
8. Do you think Lenore was jealous of Bessie?

Acknowledgments

I'm so blessed to belong to the terrific HarperCollins Christian Publishing dream team! I've been with my great fiction team for fourteen years, and they are like family to me. I learn something new with every book, which makes writing so much fun for me!

Our fiction publisher, Daisy Hutton, is a gale-force wind of fresh air. She thinks outside the box, and I love the way she empowers me and my team. The last two books have been with my terrific editor, Amanda Bostic, who really gets suspense and has been my friend from the moment I met her all those years ago. Fabulous cover guru Kristen Ingebretson works hard to create the perfect cover—and does. And, of course, I can't forget the other friends in my amazing fiction family: Becky Monds, Becky Philpott, Kristen Golden, Karli Jackson, Samantha Buck, Paul Fisher, and Stephen Tindal. You are all such a big part of my life. I wish I could name all the great folks at HCCP who work on selling my books through different venues. I'm truly blessed!

ACKNOWLEDGMENTS

Julee Schwarzburg is a dream editor to work with. She totally gets romantic suspense, and our partnership is pure joy. She brought some terrific ideas to the table with this book—as always!

My agent, Karen Solem, has helped shape my career in many ways, and that includes kicking an idea to the curb when necessary. We are about to celebrate fifteen years together! And my critique partner of seventeen years, Denise Hunter, is the best sounding board ever. Thanks, friends!

I'm so grateful for my husband, Dave, who carts me around from city to city, washes towels, and chases down dinner without complaint. My kids—Dave, Kara (and now Donna and Mark)—love and support me in every way possible, and my little granddaughter Alexa makes every day a joy. She's talking like a grown-up now, and having her spend the night is more fun than I can tell you.

Most important, I give my thanks to God, who has opened such amazing doors for me and makes the journey a golden one.

About the Author

RITA finalist Colleen Coble is the author of several bestselling romantic suspense novels, including *Tidewater Inn*, and the Mercy Falls, Lonestar, and Rock Harbor series.

Visit her website at www.colleencoble.com

Twitter: @colleencoble

Facebook: colleencoblebooks

Enjoy an excerpt from Colleen Coble's

Butterfly Palace

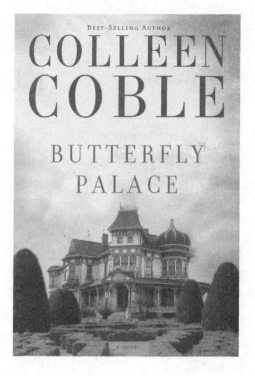

Prologue

Larson, Texas, 1900

Lily Donaldson tiptoed to the front door and winced when it opened with a creak. The last thing she wanted was to awaken her mother who was sleeping down the hall. Even though Lily was over twenty years old, her mother would take a switch to her if she knew she was sneaking out like this. The lights still shone from the livery attached to their house.

She peeked in the window as she passed. Her father sat at the desk with his partner as they pored over figures for the new expansion. There was a stack of money on the desk beside them. She stared for a moment at the stack of cash. It must have been a good day for the livery. It would be hours before their meeting came to an end. The talk of a new livery in the next town over had been going on for several weeks, and both men never seemed to tire of the topic.

The night air touched her heated skin, and she shivered as she hurried along the path to the barn. Crickets chirped as if to keep time to the ragtime tune tinkling from the tavern's piano down the street. The threat of discovery added another thump to her pulse.

The familiar scent of hay and horse greeted her when she stepped into the darkened building. "Andy?" She twisted the unfamiliar weight of the engagement ring on her finger. Her lips curved when Andy Hawkins stepped from the shadows. "I thought maybe you hadn't been able to slip away." She kept her voice barely above a whisper while she drank in his appearance.

He was a good head taller than most men, and his bulk made her feel tiny—and protected. His dark hair curled at the nape of his neck, and his eyes were the color of a buckeye nut.

His white teeth flashed below his perfect Roman nose. "I told Pa I wasn't feeling well. I'd much rather be with you." His warm hands came down on her shoulders, and he pulled her close for a kiss. "That meeting will go on for hours."

Heat ran through her at his words. She'd tried to resist the pull of their passion—they both had—but they'd been weak, so weak. The firm press of his fingers closed around her hand, and he pulled her to a comfortable stack of hay. She fell into his arms without a protest. His lips came down on hers, and she forgot everything but his touch.

He lifted his head and sniffed. "Do you smell smoke?"

Cries of alarm began to filter into her consciousness, muddied by the feel and scent of Andy. He helped her to her feet, and they both rushed to the door to view a scene that made her shudder.

Fire shot through the roof of the livery. "Pa!" Andy restrained her when she would have rushed forward.

More shouts came from town, and a line of men burst from the saloon and ran toward the burning building. The windows of the livery exploded, spewing broken glass onto the ground, then smoke poured from open frames.

Andy grabbed her hand, and they ran toward her front door.

She stopped and stared at the fire. Which direction? Her mother was in the house. Their fathers were in the livery. Lily's chest was tight as flames consumed the livery.

Her fingers closed around the doorknob. "I'll get my mother. You get the men." The metal was already hot to the touch. How could the fire have grown so quickly?

She yanked open the door and plunged inside. Thick, roiling smoke choked Lily's nose and throat as soon as she reached the top of the stairs. She threw open the bedroom door and rushed to the bed. The smoke was thick in the bedroom too. Her mother slept, unaware of the danger.

Lily shook her. "Mama, wake up! You have to get out of here." Shouts and screams echoed from outside. What was happening to her father?

Her mother lifted her head and her eyes went wide, then cleared of confusion. She threw back the covers, then stumbled to the door with Lily. One hand around her mother's waist, Lily led her down the steps. Her chest burned both with the hot smoke and the need to escape.

"Almost there," she told her mother. She reached blindly for the door, and her fingers grasped the knob. She threw open the door.

The first brush of fresh air on her skin made her gasp and draw in the thick smoke. She coughed at the searing pain in her chest, then stumbled onto the porch with her mother. Lily led her mother a safe distance away before turning to see bright flames shooting into the night. A fire alarm clanged behind them, and the horses pulling the fire engine raced around the corner. As soon as it came to a stop, the firemen leaped into the yard and ran for the livery.

Her mother coughed and stared at the furiously burning structure. "Where's your father?"

But Lily didn't see her father's bald head. Dread congealed in her belly, and she shook her head. "I don't see them, but Andy went to get them out." She stared at the throng around the building. Was that Andy?

His soot-blackened face came into view by the light of the flames. He struggled with the two men holding him. "Let go of me! I have to find them."

"It's too dangerous," one of the men said. "The place is fully engulfed."

"Stay here, Mama." Lily hurried to Andy's side. "You didn't find them?" Her throat closed at the hopeless expression on his face.

She turned to stare at the inferno that had overrun both the livery and the attached house. The fire's heat scorched her face. The breeze blew stinging cinders against her skin. Andy renewed his efforts to free himself, but the firemen propelled him back to a safer distance.

The fire's roar was like a dragon from a fairy tale, monstrous and all-consuming. Flames licked out of the upper windows, straining toward the roof. More glass shattered, and the stink of burning bedding rolled over the lawn. With a groan, the building began to sag. The firemen shoved them back even more, and they all turned to watch it give a final shudder before the weakened timbers collapsed. Sparks and flames shot higher as the fire fed on the night air and began to consume the last of the building.

Lily sank to her knees, and Andy fell with her. They held one another as the fire took their fathers.

Andy stiffened, then pulled away. "It's my fault. I should have been there. I would have smelled it and gotten them out."

"It went too fast, Andy. There was nothing any of us could do." She tried to cup his face in her hands, but he flinched away, then jumped to his feet.

"Don't look at me. I can't even stand myself." He stalked off, and the dark swallowed him up.

One

Austin, Texas, 1904

The train's whistle sounded as mournful as she felt as it pulled away from the station, leaving her on the siding with her valise at her feet. Lily brushed ineffectively at the soot on her serviceable gray skirt and squinted in the October sunshine. What if her new employer had sent no one to meet her? She didn't know how to get to her destination.

A dray pulled by two fine horses went past, and the driver stared too boldly for her taste, so she directed her gaze to her dusty black boots.

"Miss?"

She jerked her gaze back up to see a man dressed in a brown suit. A lock of reddish hair dipped below his stylish bowler. He appeared to be in his late thirties and was quite handsome.

He tipped his hat and nodded toward her luggage. "Is that all you have? You *are* Lily Donaldson?"

"Yes, yes, I am. You are from the Butterfly Palace?"

He picked up her valise and gave a vague nod her way. "This way."

People flowed around her as she followed his broad back to a fine automobile at the street. She hung back when he opened the door. "You didn't mention your name."

Amusement lit his pale blue eyes. "I'm not the killer attacking women here if that's what you're worried about."

She glanced around at the men loitering nearby. No one seemed to pay her any notice. "There's a killer?"

He shrugged. "A city is never as safe as it looks. Are you coming or not? I don't care either way. Mother asked me to fetch you when I objected to being forced to attend another of her boring balls, and I obliged. It's on your own head if you're late."

When he started for the driver's seat, she hoisted herself onto the plush seat. "I'm coming."

He grinned, and heat flared in her cheeks at his bold stare. His expensive suit proclaimed him to be much more than a driver sent to collect her. He'd mentioned his mother, so she assumed he was a Marshall.

The jerk of the automobile threw her against the leather seat and ended her speculation. It felt good to be away from the curious stares she'd endured on the train. Women didn't travel alone. She took off her bonnet and swiped some loose strands back into place, then replaced her hat.

She stared eagerly out the window at Austin. The state

capital. It was much grander than she'd imagined. Electric trolley cars zipped by so fast they made her woozy. Houses larger than four or five homes back in Larson turned stately faces toward the wide street. Mercantile shops, printers, meat markets, and dress shops passed in a dizzying blur. Where did one start to find needed items? There were too many shops to choose from.

The scent of lilacs blew away the stench of the train's coal dust that lingered on her clothing. Her pulse beat hard and fast in her neck. Her new life was about to begin, and she had no idea what to expect. While she hoped to find a new life here, the recent death of her mother left her expecting only more heartache. Still, she had to support herself even if life seemed hard and dreary.

Didn't God care? She'd never expected him to let such terrible things happen. Ever since the fire, life had spiraled down in a disheartening whirlpool of pain.

The automobile stopped in front of a grand stone mansion illuminated by electric lights. The cobblestone drive was smooth under her shoes when the man assisted her out of the back. Lily stood, absorbing the huge edifice that would have been more at home on a French mountainside. Seeing it here on Texas soil felt wrong somehow, and something about the structure was off-putting in spite of its grandeur. Maybe it was the way the windows in the mansard roof seemed to leer down at her, or perhaps it was the dark brick that made it look stern and unwelcoming. A chill shuddered down her spine, but she picked up her valise. It would surely be more attractive in the daylight.

The man shut the automobile door behind her. "Welcome to Butterfly Palace, Lily."

His forwardness in addressing her by her Christian name made her straighten. "Why is it called that?" She craned her neck again and willed herself to admire the four-story mansion.

"My stepfather is a great collector of exotic butterflies. He employs a man to bring him the finest in the world. The sunroom is filled with them, and frescoes can be found everywhere." He pointed. "You'll want to go around back to the staff entrance, but I'm sure we'll be seeing more of one another. The name's Lambreth. I suppose I'll inherit this monstrosity someday." He winked at her.

The instructions and his wink took her aback. There was little distinction between servant and master in Larson, but then, no one in her hometown put on airs or flashed their wealth around. She took a step toward the side of the house, but Mr. Lambreth touched her arm and motioned her in the other direction.

"I'll have Rollo bring in your trunk. Mrs. O'Reilly will tell you where you're sleeping. See you around."

"Thank you." Gathering her courage, Lily followed a cobblestone path around the west side of the house.

Light spilled into a rose garden from large windows along the side of the house. Lily stopped and gaped. Women in shimmering silk dresses mingled with men in formal attire under a spectacular gas chandelier. The opulent scene was like something from *Godey's*. Houseboys and maids carrying trays offered food and drink to the guests, and piano music tinkled out the open windows.

She reined in her impulse to run back to the automobile and ask to be returned to the train. This life was far outside her experience, and she'd never fit in here. Would she be expected to wear a black dress and white apron and cap?

Tightening her grip on her small valise, she forced herself forward to the back door. The aroma of roast beef mingled with fish and cake as she knocked on the door.

The door opened, and a slim woman about Lily's age peered out. Her hazel eyes sparkled with life above flushed cheeks. "You must be Lily. I expected you an hour ago. We need you." She reached out and yanked the valise from Lily's hand. "We're shorthanded. Your dress will do for now, but take off your hat and put on an apron."

She left the door standing open and stepped back into a hall that opened into a large kitchen. Lily followed the young woman into the kitchen where the cooking odors grew stronger. The aromas of beef and fish vied with that of cinnamon and apples. Food covered a scarred wooden table, and several servants bustled around the room.

A tiny woman dressed in black orchestrated the chaos. The red hair under her cap was coiled in a bun tight enough to give her a headache. Her brown eyes assessed Lily, and she nodded. "So you're Lily?" Her brogue told of her Irish heritage. "I'm Glenda O'Reilly, the housekeeper. You may call me Mrs. O'Reilly."

"What would you have me do tonight?"

Mrs. O'Reilly pointed to a shelf and pegs. "Hang up your hat there. Emily, get her an apron."

The young woman who had opened the door nodded and reached into a cupboard. She handed a white apron to Lily. "You can take around the cider."

Lily pulled the pins from her hat and placed it on the shelf, then tied the apron around her waist. "You're Emily?"

The young woman nodded. "Sorry, love, I didn't introduce myself, did I? We'll be roommates, and there will be time to get acquainted later. *After* the party."

Lily's chest felt tight, and she wished she'd hidden out in the rose garden until the party was over. "When am I to meet Mrs. Marshall?"

"Tomorrow." Mrs. O'Reilly's brow lifted in challenge as if daring Lily to object.

"Yes, ma'am. I am just to offer the guests cider? I'll do my best."

"That's all I ask." The housekeeper pointed to a large tray filled with fine blue-and-white china cups. "Smile and let the guests take their own cup of mulled cider. Try not to spill it. When your tray is empty, come back here and get more."

Like Joan of Arc going to the stake, Lily squared her shoulders and picked up the tray.

❧

Women in shimmering silks of every imaginable color danced by on the arms of men in sleek black suits. A mural over the fireplace depicted a butterfly in beautiful hues of blue and yellow. Drew

Hawkes hung back in the corner and idly listened to the conversations around him, mostly about the recent murder of a servant girl. The unfortunate young woman had been discovered a few blocks from here, and the entire city was in a state. This was the third murder in two months.

Everett Marshall motioned to Drew, and he left the sanctuary of his corner to join him. Everett clapped a hand on Drew's shoulder. "This is the young man I was telling you about. Drew is quite gifted with investments, and you would do well to employ him. Drew, this is Stuart Vesters. He owns the stockyard on the west side of town." Drew shook the man's hand, noticing the lack of enthusiasm in Stuart's grip. "Pleased to meet you, Mr. Vesters. I'm not currently taking on more clients though, sir. I'd be happy to put you on a waiting list." Dangling the carrot just out of reach tended to be much more effective than a hard sell.

Sure enough, the older man squared his shoulders and lifted a brow. "When could we discuss it, Mr. Hawkes? I might be persuaded to change investment companies. Everett here has been singing your praises for more than a month."

"I'm booked through the next three weeks, but I'd be happy to make an appointment after Thanksgiving." Drew had been trying to get close to Vesters for nearly six months. It wouldn't do to appear too eager. His supervisor wouldn't be happy if he ruined things now.

"That's much too far. I have some time on Thursday. We can meet in town."

Drew eyed the man's set jaw and read his determination. Good. "Let me see if I can rearrange my schedule." He whipped out a black leather calendar and pretended to peruse it. He pulled out a pencil and acted as though he were erasing something. "I can make that work. My other client may squawk, but I'll make it up to him with a new tip."

Vesters smiled with self-satisfaction, and Drew allowed himself a small smile as the man reached for a glass of cider. Drew looked at the young woman holding the tray. He blinked and looked again. All the blood drained from his head, and his knees went weak as he took in the blond hair and pointed chin.

Lily? It wasn't possible. She hadn't seen him yet as her attention was on Vesters. Drew's gaze drank in the face he'd seen only in his dreams for four years. Those delicate features and smooth skin hadn't changed in all this time. Her eyes were such a dark blue, and they grew even darker when she was angry. The glorious hair he'd loved to see released from its pins was hidden under an ugly maid's cap. The years had brought a new maturity to her beauty.

Drew turned on his heels and melted into the crowd. His pulse throbbed in his throat. He had to calm himself. If Vesters smelled something off now, it could ruin the whole thing. He spared a glance back at the group, but she wasn't looking his way. Maybe she hadn't seen him.

What was Lily doing here, so far from Larson? She wore an apron like she was a maid. Part of him longed to rush to her and announce himself. Did she hate him? He deserved it after the way he'd left without a word.

He was in the middle of the dancing couples, so he cut in on the man squiring Belle Castle. "I hope you don't mind, Miss Castle."

"Not at all, Mr. Hawkes." She flashed him a coy smile.

He'd known for weeks that the beautiful brunette held some fondness for him, and he hated to encourage it now, but Everett would be happy to see him dancing with his niece and would unlikely be upset at Drew's sudden departure. Everett would smooth things over with Vesters.

Drew was so distracted he didn't notice when the musicians struck up a reel. Belle picked up her pace but he didn't. Their feet became entangled. He tried to catch his balance, but everything was happening too fast. He released Belle so she wouldn't share his disgrace. In the moment he scrambled away, his arm collided with the soft body of someone behind him. The deep red Oriental rug rose to meet him, and they both went down in a tangle of limbs. The contents of the china cups darkened the red carpet to deep garnet.

The rest of the dancers stopped and stared. Someone snickered, and heat rose to his face. He quickly flipped the lady's dress over her lower limbs and sprang to his feet. "I'm terribly sorry. I–I–" His apology died when he stared into Lily's scarlet face.

Her eyes were wide and horrified. "Andy?"

He hadn't heard that nickname since his father died. "I'll explain later," he said low enough that only she could hear. After helping her to her feet, he knelt and put the cups back on the tray. Some of them were broken, and he prayed she wasn't blamed for the encounter.

She hadn't left when he stood with the tray in his hands. The rest of the guests began to move off, and the music tinkled out again.

Knowing his duty, he glanced at Belle. "I'm so sorry, Miss Castle. You are unharmed?"

"I'm fine, Mr. Hawkes." Belle smiled, and the amusement lit her eyes with a warm glow. "That was a much-needed bit of excitement for this too-dull party. I do believe I'll take my leave though and attend to my dress." She gestured to dark splotches on her gown. He opened his mouth to apologize again, but she held up her hand. "No harm done. I'll see you tomorrow for dinner."

He gave a slight bow. "I shall look forward to it."

Christopher Lambreth, Mrs. Marshall's son, gave a genial grin and held out his arm. "I'll escort you, cousin. I fear you've lost your usual fine sense of balance."

Belle laughed and took his arm. When her emerald skirt disappeared in the swirl of other gowns, Drew turned his attention back to Lily. She seemed rooted to the spot. His reappearance had to have rattled her.

He took her arm. "Let's get out of here. Make no sign that you know me."

She gave a slight nod. "Your past actions have already made it clear I don't know you at all."

His lips tightened, and he guided her through the crowd to

the blessed cool of the hall outside the ballroom. "Lily, what are you doing here?"

She jerked her arm from his grip. "I think the better question would be, what are *you* doing here, Andy? And the first question begs the second. Where have you been for the past four years and two months?"

Part of him rejoiced that she knew so clearly how long he'd been gone, but that fact also revealed the depth of the pain he'd caused. "It will take too long to explain now. Can you meet me tomorrow afternoon at the park? Say nothing about my identity to anyone."

She shook her head. "I don't think I want to hear it. And besides, I don't know what my duties are yet. I just arrived tonight." Her eyes filled with tears. "Who are you really, Andy?" She turned toward the kitchen door.

"Wait, Lily, I want to talk to you." But the swish of her skirt was the only response he received.

❦

The story continues in Colleen Coble's *Butterfly Palace*...

THE SUNSET COVE
series

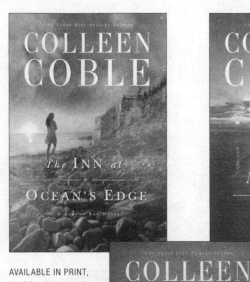

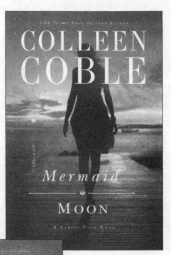

AVAILABLE IN PRINT,
E-BOOK, AND AUDIO

AVAILABLE IN PRINT,
E-BOOK, AND AUDIO

AVAILABLE IN PRINT, E-BOOK,
AND AUDIO SEPTEMBER 2016

Colleen loves to hear from her readers!

Be sure to sign up for Colleen's newsletter for insider information on deals and appearances.

Visit her website at www.colleencoble.com
Twitter: @colleencoble
Facebook: colleencoblebooks

THOMAS NELSON
Since 1798